# Word Night

## ON

# Union Station

EarthCent Ambassador Series:

Book Nine of EarthCent Ambassador


# Word Night on Union Station

Foner Books


ISBN 978-1-948691-11-6


Copyright 2016 by E. M. Foner


Northampton, Massachusetts

# One

"In conclusion, it is the view of Union Station Embassy that humans have little chance of catching up with alien manufacturing technologies as long as the majority of our technical universities are staffed by former students, and this paradigm is unlikely to—Libby!"

"Yes, Ambassador?"

"It's 'paradigm,' isn't it?"

"Are you referring to fourteen down in last Friday's Galactic Free Press crossword puzzle?"

"Don't play coy with me. Dring is coming for dinner and I've never finished a crossword puzzle before him. Sometimes I think he's making them up for Walter on the sly. What was the clue again?"

"A set of linguistic items that form mutually exclusive choices."

"Paradigm! I'm sure that's the alternative meaning. Argh, I hate working these puzzles on my heads-up display. Can you shift it to my display desk, please?"

"Very well, Ambassador, but at this rate, you're going to be late for dinner and miss your self-imposed deadline for your weekly report."

"I'll just look at it for a minute," Kelly promised. "There's something about the hints to this crossword that I can't quite put my finger on. They're much more specific

1

than usual and at least four times as long, but with 'Clive's Clues,' as the title, I was sure that the words were all going to be espionage-related." The ambassador spent a full minute staring at the hologram of the partially solved crossword puzzle that materialized over her display desk before shaking her head in disgust. "I still can't spot the pattern."

"You mean the paradigm."

"What? Oh, now you're just making fun of me. Can you play back that last paragraph before I interrupted myself so I can finish my report?" Kelly waved the hologram out of existence and rose to begin pacing back and forth behind her desk as the Stryx librarian provided her cue.

"On the bright side, humans who live on Verlock academy worlds have proven that our best brains are capable of beginning to understand much of the alien sciences, though our relatively short life spans are a serious handicap to achieving the mastery that comes with centuries of study. But the core problem, as explained to me by several technology experts, is that engineering is based on practice rather than theories. Theories may be useful in explaining why engineering works, but in and of itself, basic research does little to advance commercially useful technologies."

Kelly nodded her head in agreement with her own words, and then took a deep breath to fuel her final run-on sentence.

"In conclusion, it is the view of Union Station Embassy that humans have little chance of catching up with alien manufacturing technologies as long as the majority of our technical universities are staffed by former students, and this pa—, uh, pattern is unlikely to be broken until humans who trained in alien work environments or studied in the

2

Stryx Open University are recruited as faculty for Earth's education industry."

"Report encrypted and sent," Libby said. "I'm glad to hear you've come to that conclusion. Some of us were beginning to wonder if you were hoping that Earth's education system would fix itself, but Jeeves assured me that we could expect a paradigm shift at any time."

"I get it already. I'm sorry I interrupted my report and then made you repeat part of it back, but I do worry about what the schools are teaching on Earth. I only finished a year of university before EarthCent hired me, but even though some of my professors had been born after the Stryx came, they were still teaching what their professors had taught them. The EarthCent Intelligence assessment shows that technical education back on Earth is hopelessly outdated. According to one survey, two out of three physics professors still believe that faster-than-light travel is impossible!"

"Theory of relativity," Libby confirmed. "It has a certain beauty to it, but it's a bit constraining if you actually want to go places."

"I'll say. Paul was telling me that one of the girls he studied with at your Open University, Lin somebody, actually understands the theoretical underpinnings of early Drazen jump drives. But when she wanted to get a job teaching at an Earth university, they wouldn't even hire her as an assistant because they don't recognize your accreditation."

"The librarian on Far Station who handles administration for our Open University network did entertain an accreditation delegation from Earth some years ago. Unfortunately, talks bogged down over the delegation's insistence that we replace proficiency testing with a numbered system of prerequisites." Libby broke off her explanation and said, "You asked me to tell you when Clive arrived."

"He's here? Great! Maybe he can help me figure out the point of the crossword puzzle title."

Kelly went to her office door and swiped open the lock that she only engaged during important meetings or when filing her weekly report. She stuck her head out and scanned the reception area, but Donna had already headed home for the weekend and Clive was nowhere to be seen. Then she heard voices coming from Daniel's office and went to investigate.

"Ambassador, come in," Daniel said, beckoning her into the small room. "Clive was on his way to see you, but I hijacked him to show off my new name-plate."

"You've changed your name?"

"My title," he said proudly. Kelly looked at the holographic nameplate on her junior consul's display desk and realized that the 'Junior' was missing.

"They promoted you without telling me?" she asked in surprise.

"Well, not exactly," Daniel admitted. "I'm trying to be more proactive about my career."

"But you know that the Stryx actually control promotions for all of the higher level EarthCent positions, and I doubt they're going to be influenced by your changing the title on your nameplate."

"I had new business cards made too," Daniel said, passing one to the ambassador.

Kelly took the card and read, "EarthCent Consul – Daniel Cohan." The junior consul nodded happily. "Uh, do you think it's smart to hand these out? I always give you excellent evaluations and I'm sure you'll get a promotion eventually, but I worry something like this could backfire."

"Jeeves is the one who told me that if I wanted to get ahead I should present EarthCent and the Stryx with a fait accompli. He's been studying diplomacy, you know."

Kelly blinked, and then a smile spread over her face. "Fait accompli. Something that has already happened that you cannot change. That's seventeen across!"

"You're going around with the Galactic Free Press crossword on your heads-up display again, aren't you?" Clive accused the ambassador. "You're going to trip over something or walk through an atmosphere retention field and wind up breathing vacuum one of these days."

"I'm just trying to give Dring some real competition for a change. Besides, it's practically your fault. How did your name end up in the puzzle's title?"

Clive shrugged. "Walter knows that I don't even look at the things. Blythe got annoyed when she saw it because she thinks he's making fun of me. Her theory is that he's implying that I'd start doing crossword puzzles if the hints were obvious enough."

"I'm sure that's not it," Kelly said. "Crossword puzzle clues usually include misdirection and puns to make them more difficult. Just like you're the spy who doesn't hide his identity, Walter is probably pointing out that the hints for this week's crossword should be taken literally. The trick is that there isn't any trick, but that's exactly what it takes to confuse people like me who are expecting one."

"Before you confuse me any further, let me tell you why I'm here. We just received word that another Galactic Free Press reporter on the Sharf/Horten frontier has been kidnapped by pirates, and you told me you wanted to know immediately if it happened again."

"That's the fourth one this year," Kelly said in frustration. "Libby? Do you know anything about this?"

"The kidnapping on the Horten frontier is technically outside of the tunnel network, but I have to say that it's the sort of behavior one would expect from pirates," the Stryx librarian replied.

Clive nodded his agreement. "Blythe has invited Chastity and her senior staff to dinner for a talk about whether it's really necessary to send reporters out there."

"I can't imagine that Walter will take any interference from EarthCent Intelligence lying down, but maybe Brinda will talk some sense into him," Kelly said. "Any chance you could invite Daniel along to represent the diplomatic service?"

"I'll go anywhere if I can pass out my new cards," Daniel offered.

"Busy day," Libby interjected brightly. "President Beyer just requested a secure channel to talk with you."

"What time is it on Earth?"

"Nearly midnight, but he's asking if you could spare him a few minutes. I told him you're with Clive and Daniel and he said to bring them along."

"No time like the present," Kelly replied. "Let's go, boys. Next door."

Clive and Daniel followed Kelly into the reception area, where the junior consul grabbed an extra chair before entering the ambassador's office. Kelly swiped the door lock after them and then took her seat, just as a hologram of a very rumpled President Beyer appeared over her display desk. He was holding a tumbler of a light amber liquid with a single ice cube floating in the glass.

"Glad I caught you," the president said. "I happened to listen to your report as it came in, and putting aside the

6

odd choice of words, I think you're onto something important."

"Thank you, Mr. President," Kelly said formally. "Some of the human engineers on the station have complained to me that they want to help Earth move forward with new manufacturing techniques but they're being shut out by credentialing issues."

The president seemed distracted as Kelly replied and made a shooing away gesture at somebody who didn't appear in the hologram. Then he took another sip from his drink and assumed a thoughtful expression, which Kelly took as an invitation to continue.

"I've also just learned that another Galactic Free Press reporter has been kidnapped by pirates, though I wouldn't put it past the Grenouthians to be involved."

"There's not much we can do to protect humans who go off the tunnel network looking for trouble," the president said. "Hell, there's not much we can do to protect humans anywhere, if you'll pardon my French."

"So why did you call, Mr. President?"

The president took another sip of his Scotch, causing the ice cube to make a seductive tinkling sound, and Kelly could almost see him coming to a decision. He set down the tumbler and massaged his temples for a moment before sharing his thoughts.

"The reason I contacted you tonight is because I want to visit Union Station as soon as possible. I know it's difficult to keep anything a secret these days, so if your embassy can manage a reception on short notice, it won't look like I'm trying to sneak around. Maybe I'll present an award to the newspaper for their investigative journalism while I'm there. Does EarthCent give out medals?" he asked his off-hologram companion. "No? Well, I don't imagine they cost very much so it's about time we started. I could give one to that children's show host at the same time. It will be good for EarthCent's brand recognition."

"We'd be happy to have you, of course," Kelly said, wondering how the subject had shifted from piracy to children's programming.

"Why not let your junior consul take care of the reception?" the president suggested. "I'm told he's done a great job with the sovereign human communities conferences. The delegations from open worlds who have visited Earth looking for money in the last couple years always speak highly of him."

"Thank you, Mr. President," Daniel said, sensing his opportunity. "It's Consul Cohan now."

"Oh, you've been promoted? I don't remember seeing the paperwork."

"Must have gotten lost, Mr. President," Daniel asserted. "Could you put it in again for me?"

"Take a note," the president said to his off-hologram companion. "Then I look forward to seeing all three of you in a few weeks. Was there anything else?" The president turned to his invisible assistant again and squinted as though he were trying to read something that was printed too small. "Okay, I need to wrap this up and get going. And tell that Walter fellow to stop making up such impossible crossword puzzles or I'm cancelling my subscription."

The hologram dissolved before anybody could respond.

"Do you think he went for it?" Daniel asked. "He did tell her to take a note."

"Your fait accompli?" Kelly shook her head. "It's midnight there and he had a drink in his hand so he may see things differently in the morning. Besides, how do you

8

know that it was a woman and not a man in the room with him?"

"He's married. He wouldn't have hidden a man."

"You're going to be late for dinner," Libby reminded the ambassador.

"That's right," Kelly declared, rising from her chair. "Will you lock up, Daniel? I've got to get home."

As the ambassador headed for the lift tube, it occurred to her that this was the first time she could remember leaving the embassy before Daniel on a Friday afternoon. Maybe his "promotion" had brought with it a new sense of responsibility.

The smells of Aisha's cooking greeted her when she entered the ice harvester, but the table hadn't been set, and it looked like the rest of the family was running late as well. A chubby little dinosaur browsing through her book shelves looked over when she entered.

"Dring," Kelly said warmly. "Do you have any idea where everybody is?"

"Aisha is in the kitchen with Fenna, but Paul got hung up at Libbyland and he's going to be late. Joe is working on a small cabin cruiser just on the other side of the training grounds. He said he'd be along any minute, and he asked me to tell you that Dorothy volunteered to cover a shift at the lost-and-found for a Fillinduck girl who suddenly molted out of season. Your son is playing in his room with Banger, and Beowulf is keeping an eye on them."

"Thank you, Dring. You're saving us a fortune in ping charges."

"Did you enjoy this week's puzzle?" the Maker asked.

Kelly grimaced and flopped down in her Love-U massaging recliner. "I was sure I was going to finish this one but I got hung up in the section with all the words derived from Greek and French. I did figure out the meaning of the title, though, so you should give me partial credit. It's an allusion to Clive's job as the head of EarthCent Intelligence being the worst-kept secret in the galaxy."

"Hmm. I interpreted it differently but perhaps Walter fooled me this time."

The shape-shifter began unrolling a large sheet of parchment on which he had drawn the previous Friday's crossword puzzle and then filled in all of the blanks with ink calligraphy. He always presented his solution to Kelly before the solved puzzle was released with the new challenge on Friday night. After a few days, the ink Dring employed would turn into a fine dust and release from the scroll, allowing Kelly to return the parchment to him for reuse.

"What did you make of the title?" Kelly asked, suddenly unsure of her own solution.

"I'm sure you recognized that the verbose hints this week were all partial definitions from the Oxford English Dictionary. I memorized it back when I was learning your delightful language."

"Of course," Kelly groaned, resisting the urge to slap herself on the forehead. "Clive Oxford. Clive's Clues. How could I miss that, especially after Blythe explained how he took the name from an English clothing boutique." Kelly shook her head sadly. "So it turns out that the title was just as straightforward as the hints. I was looking for a riddle wrapped in a mystery inside an enigma, but it turned out to be a reference work I have on my shelf."

Kelly got up and went to retrieve her recently acquired two-volume boxed edition of the dictionary to show it off to Dring. Despite the fact that she could instantly look up any word in any language on her heads-up display, she'd always coveted the condensed Oxford English Dictionary with its tiny print and the large magnifying glass in the cardboard drawer above the books. Her mother had located a century-old set at an estate sale on Earth and sent it in the diplomatic pouch for Kelly's fifty-third birthday.

"Is something wrong?" Dring asked.

Kelly stood stock still in front of a largish gap on the bookshelf, a tragic expression on her face. "I forgot I loaned it to somebody two weeks ago," she muttered.

"Walter?"

"Brinda. He must have put her up to it. Do you think this is fair grounds to ask them to return the wedding present I gave them?"

"What was it?"

"A big dog bowl and some industrial-strength chew toys. I'm sure Beowulf wouldn't mind that they've been used by that pretty Cayl hound Brinda brought back from her imperial hostage experience."

"Interesting choice for a wedding present."

"Don't you remember? They insisted that people only give them things from the bridal registry that she set up at the Shuk. I think she was afraid that people would buy them decorative items that she didn't want to display. She studied art history, you know."

"Ah, you're correct. I spoke without thinking," the Maker admitted. "I ended up giving them a variety of cleaning products. Very practical."

Aisha stuck her head out of the kitchen and looked around the room. "You're home. I started cooking late because Paul's hung up at work and Dorothy is skipping. I gave Samuel a sandwich when he got back from dance practice."

"Thank you, Aisha. By the way, the president of EarthCent is planning an official visit to Union Station and he wants to present you with a medal."

"Does he intend to do it on my show for publicity? I'd have to check with the Grenouthians first. There was some specific language in the contract about letting politicians appear and I'd hate to have to give equal time to the other species. The children would find it awfully boring."

# Two

Dorothy sat on the counter of the lost-and-found, grilling Flazint about the details of the Frunge girl's latest suitor. "And then he gave you a grow-lamp for your birthday?"

"It's specially tuned for hair vines," Flazint replied. "Our deck lighting is alright for most things, but it doesn't penetrate to the roots the way focused infrared does. It's not just for the vines, either. Frunge who try to get by on the deck lighting usually end up with dry scalps, and you know what that means."

"Dandruff." Dorothy nodded knowledgably. "But isn't a grow-lamp like a serious commitment? Do you think he's going to pop the question?"

"You mean, ask his parents to ask my parents to ask our ancestors to ask his ancestors to make an offer?"

"Uh, I guess. Do you mean your ancestors have veto power over who you get to marry?"

"Of course," Flazint said. "Do you mean that Humans make their children do everything themselves? Unless you've been married before, how would you know what contract terms to ask for?"

"Contract?"

Flazint stared at Dorothy in disbelief. "Are you saying that Humans get married without negotiating a contract first? How do you know who is responsible for what?"

13

"I guess some humans have contracts, like religious things. But I believe that as long as there's love, everything else will work itself out."

"Wow! You guys really are backwards. No offense, I mean," she added hastily. "So are you serious with this David guy?"

"I don't know. I only turned eighteen last week and I'm not in any hurry. My mom didn't marry until she was thirty-five."

"And you guys live to, what? Three hundred? Four hundred?"

"More like eighty or ninety," Dorothy said, sounding a bit embarrassed at her deficient longevity. "Libby says that in a few hundred thousand years, we'll probably live just as long as the Frunge or the Drazens, but the only way to do it now is with yucky tech stuff."

"I didn't know," Flazint said, tapping her own chin with a knuckle, the deepest apology gesture used by her people. "We didn't do Human biology in school. I always thought it was because of anti-Human bias, but now I wonder if they just didn't want to shock us. Anyway, I guess that explains your courting."

"What do you mean?"

"You don't have any time to waste. Our contract negotiations for a marriage can stretch out for decades. You visited my family's house. Don't you remember the way my ancestors talked?"

"It was more like groaning. Really slow."

"And they aren't ambulatory, so it all has to be done through sending messages back and forth. Most families use the shrubs for that, and I'm sure you can imagine how unreliable kids are at that age. It's like playing the old

14

classroom game where children in a circle whisper a message to each other and it comes back all garbled."

"I guess every species has its own problems. Anyway, thanks for agreeing to cover for me while I'm poking around out back. Libby gave permission for a friend to come and help me, but Chance has a bit of an issue with showing up on time."

"Didn't you say that she's an artificial person? How is she going to help with your fashion project?"

"Chance is the most stylish sentient I've ever met, and that includes the Vergallians who show up for Mom's embassy parties. She also knows a lot about travel clothes and accessories because she was always on the move in her early years when she was, er..." Dorothy trailed off after failing to come up with a diplomatic way to express that the artificial person had skipped out on her body mortgage payments.

"You're so lucky that you can design your own curriculum at the Open University," Flazint said enviously. "My ancestors and my parents choose all of the courses for me. I'll be lucky if I can take some electives in my last year."

"But I thought you wanted to be a metallurgist. You always sound so excited when you tell me you spotted a new alien alloy in some item that shows up in the bins."

"I do, but I wish we had more hands-on work, like the cool bags and dresses you're always making. So far it's all materials science and chemistry, with a little engineering thrown in just to make the tests harder. I want to drop forge something!"

"I have to take theory courses too," Dorothy commiserated. "Do I really need to know the difference between additive color and subtractive color to design a handbag? And even when I get to make something for school, it has

15

to be so precise, and then I have to record all of the fiddly little details like it's a lab experiment. If I wanted black polish a few years ago, I went to the Shuk and bought a can for two creds. Last week I had to go to a certified manufacturing supplier, and they're like, 'We need the color coordinates,' and I'm like, 'Black, please,' but the Dollnick clerk just turned his back on me and walked away."

"They're so rude," Flazint sympathized.

"So I pull up the color theory course addendum on my tab, and it turns out that humans have four different systems for color coordinates, none of which even translate directly into Dollnick. So I call the clerk back, and I'm like, 'Just give me the blackest one, all zeros.' He brings out this little can, a tenth of the size of what I'd get at the Shuk, and charges me twelve creds! When I get home and open it, there's no pigment at all. It's completely clear."

"What happened then?"

"Well, I checked with Libby, and it turns out that there's a standard pigment system used by all of the alien manufacturers which defines colors by what you put in, so all zeros is supposed to be clear. But I know that Dollnick understood what I wanted."

"Ouch," Flazint said. "At least it wasn't a big can. I never would have guessed that polish or paint could be as technical as steel."

"Anyway, I'm not really that interested in the manufacturing end, but everybody except for Chance says that I have to study it or I could end up designing stuff that can't be produced commercially. I mean, if I can make it myself, doesn't that prove that it's doable?"

"Well, they have a point," the Frunge girl said. "I could start with a block of silver and file it into the shape of a spoon, but you wouldn't want to go into business making cutlery that way."

"Maybe not," Dorothy admitted. "But the really high-end stuff usually is hand-crafted, and if you can earn as much selling one bespoke spoon as a thousand mass-manufactured ones, you'll save a lot on packaging materials."

"That's how I look at it," Chance declared, hopping onto the counter from the customer side. She was testing the stealth-mode upgrade Thomas had ordered on trial evaluation from Quick-U, and neither of the girls had heard the artificial person enter the lost-and-found. Chance swung her legs over the counter, showing off a new pair of Vergallian walking heels in the process, and ended up sitting side-by-side with Dorothy. The two of them looked like classmates.

"Wow, great shoes," Flazint said. "I wish I could wear something like that, but our feet are a bit, you know."

"A bit rooty," Chance completed the Frunge girl's thought. "Still, it's better than being a Verlock female. They weigh so much that they can't wear heels for fear that they'll poke holes in the deck."

"That's not true," Dorothy scolded her friend. "And I don't see why a few vestigial roots should keep you from wearing stylish shoes, Flazint. You don't have to add dirt to them anymore, do you?"

"Not since I was a shrub," the Frunge girl confirmed.

"So why do all of your shoes look like construction boots?"

"I guess I never really thought about it. We kind of focus on our hair vines because that's what the guys notice."

"Males have no fashion sense whatsoever," Chance declared. "Thomas only owns two pairs of dancing shoes, and even that's just because I bought him the second pair after I caught him trying to cover scuff marks on the old ones with my black lipstick."

"Ugh," both of the girls said together.

"What's worse is that he doesn't even notice my shoes unless I grind a heel into his toe to make him look. I mean, when we were shopping for a place to move in together, he wouldn't even agree to a walk-in closet."

"But you found a place a year ago," Dorothy said. "What did you do with all your stuff?"

"I convinced him we needed a two-bedroom in case the relationship didn't work out, and then I commandeered one bedroom for a closet," Chance explained.

"So what are you guys hoping to find on the old shelves?" Flazint asked. "If you go back more than three rows, there won't even be any human stuff because you weren't part of the tunnel network back then."

"It's sort of my grandmother's idea," Dorothy said. "She told me that when she married my grandfather, he had a couple of suits passed down from his grandfather that he kept in mothballs. Human men have this weird theory that fashions just repeat themselves, so if you hold on to well-made clothes long enough they'll come back into style again."

"So you do get career guidance from your ancestors," Flazint said, nodding her head in approval.

"Did your grandfather ever get to wear those suits?" Chance asked.

"Not if my grandmother had anything to say about it. But the point is, the lost-and-found shelves hold samples from almost six thousand years of alien fashions. I thought it would make an interesting research paper to see how they changed over that time and whether any of them really did repeat."

"Cool," Flazint said. "Let me know if you need anything from the cataloging system, Chance. I don't think it will respond to your voice because you're not an employee. Did Dorothy explain the system?"

"Maybe once or twice," the artificial person said, winking at the Frunge girl. "Shall we start by going back a couple hundred years at a time? Most alien fashions don't change that fast, though the Vergallians are the exception that makes the rule."

Dorothy led Chance around the side of the track system for the shelves and counted off four 'S' curves before turning into a loop. The shelving units were one-sided, like bookcases, so there were full shelves on both sides of the aisle. If they had entered the loops from the other side of the room, they would have seen nothing but the closed backs of the shelving units.

"Remember," Dorothy cautioned the artificial person, who had already begun rummaging through the lower shelves. "Anything you pull off the shelf you have to put back exactly where you found it or it will get lost. If you're not sure what something is and you want to find out, just make a note of the shelving location and then we can ask the cataloging system."

"Check this out," Chance said, pulling a glittering red cloak from the shelf. The elegant garment might have been constructed from tiny links of a copper alloy, like an eveningwear version of chainmail. "I saw a humanoid wearing one of these in an orbital bar one time, though I can't remember the species." The artificial person twirled once or twice to show off the cloak, then tossed it carelessly back into a random opening.

"Is that where you found it?" Dorothy asked nervously.

"What? Oh, maybe not. Let's see, I think—a formal ball gown!" Chance interrupted herself, pulling a silky black dress from the shelf. She held it against her front, and the cloth flowed over the artificial person's ample curves like a liquid. "It's practically my size too. Can I have it? Libby, will you sell it to me?"

"That chainmail cloak is from location ISA 63/2, Dorothy," the Stryx librarian said, pointedly ignoring the artificial person. "You did promise to keep things tidy."

"I'll do it, I'll do it." Chance retrieved the red metal cloak and put it back in the proper spot. "Now can I please have this gown?" she pleaded. "I've never seen anything like it. I can't believe any woman could have left it behind accidentally so she must have died or something."

"You heard how the system works," Libby responded. "Tell Flazint where you found it and we'll trace the ownership chain."

Chance practically sprinted for the front counter, moving amazingly fast in her heels.

"Don't encourage her," Dorothy said to Libby, as she followed her artificial friend at a more sedate pace. "This wasn't supposed to be a shopping trip."

"Trust me," Libby replied mysteriously.

Flazint was just finishing up with a customer when Dorothy reached the front desk. Chance waited impatiently at the cataloging turntable with the liquid black gown.

"I found it at JOB 40/13," the artificial person said, handing the dress to the Frunge girl.

Flazint half-placed, half-poured the liquid-like cloth onto the turntable, and instructed the cataloging system, "Identify object from JOB 40/13."

"Sharf death shroud."

"Ew," Flazint said, backing away from the turntable and turning to Chance. "You pick it up."

Chance shook her head vigorously from side to side.

"Libby?" Dorothy asked. "Do you have imaging from when the gown was discovered? Is it, uh, used?"

"Low resolution only," Libby replied, and a grainy hologram popped into view over the turntable. A Sharf corpse was shown lying on a gurney, dressed in a liquid black gown that detailed every protruding rib. Her wilted eyestalks slumped almost to the neckline. A number of somber mourners surrounded the deceased.

"Double ew," Chance squealed, moving further away.

The hologram continued to play, showing the body being loaded into a sort of a launching tube feet-first. There was a whooshing noise, the light over the tube door turned green, and the party of mourners moved away.

"Fast forwarding," Libby said.

The scene didn't change, but a maintenance bot came into the picture and opened the ejection tube door. The black garment practically poured out onto the floor. The bot looked at it for a moment, and then looked into the tube, as if it was considering putting the shroud back where it came from and flushing it into space. Then the bot reached down with a pincer and the hologram blinked out.

"Is it safe to handle?" Dorothy asked in resignation.

"Yes," Libby said. "You wouldn't be affected by Sharf pathogens even if they were fresh, and the gown has been on the shelves for over two hundred years. But it's clear it will never be claimed, so you can just tip it into one of the blue bins and let the bots recycle it. Unless you still want it, Chance," the Stryx librarian offered disingenuously.

"Ugh," the artificial person said. "I'll be back in a minute. I'm going to find somewhere to wash my hands."

Dorothy sighed and picked up the blue recycling bin, holding it against the edge of the counter with her body. Then she took a crumpled ball of aluminum foil that one of the bots had mistaken as potential treasure and used it to scrape the gown off the turntable and into the bin.

By the end of Flazint's shift, Dorothy and a much-subdued Chance had identified a fashion trend in Horten millinery that neither of them would have noticed without six thousand years of widely spaced samples. The basic shape of the hats had changed very little, mainly variations in the crown, but what started as a veil on the front, slowly evolved into a split veil. From there, it became a half-veil with a half-hatband, then a full hatband with no veil, then a hatband with a tail, then a double-tail with no hatband. Successive generations of Horten milliners had succeeded in creating demand for new products without changing the materials needed to make a hat.

"Next time we'll look at travel accessories," Dorothy told Chance. "We can stick with the stuff that you can see on the shelves until you're ready to start touching things again."

"I'll get over it, I just need something to cheer me up," the artificial person said. "Which reminds me, there's a party this weekend some of my dance friends are throwing. It'll be lots of artists and musicians. Both of you should come."

"Can I bring David too?" Dorothy asked immediately.

"Of course, they welcome everybody. You might want to warn him to bring his nose plugs, though."

"Is there something wrong with the air?"

"If they're artists, maybe they don't bathe," Flazint interjected.

"It's just that some of them smoke stuff, use vaporizers, you know," Chance explained. "They're great people, but there's a bit of a recreational drug culture going on there."

"Oh," Dorothy said. She'd heard about parties like this from her Open University classmates but none of them ever seemed to get invited. "I guess if David is willing, I should go once just to see what it's like."

"Have a good time," Flazint said. "There's no way I'm risking my hair vines at some party where people are smoking and using drug vaporizers. I've heard it stunts budding."

# Three

"Is Jeeves hiding somewhere?" Blythe asked. She ostentatiously looked under the conference table in the
EarthCent Intelligence meeting room to check if the Stryx
was lurking out of sight.

"Did you invite him?" Chastity inquired.

"It didn't occur to me to bother. He usually invites himself."

"He's been busy working with Paul at Libbyland lately,"
Thomas said. The artificial person glanced around the
table at the unusual combination of participants, which
included Tinka in her Drazen women's business suit and
Walter Dunkirk, the managing editor of the Galactic Free
Press. "Besides, Jeeves is only interested in the spy stuff,
and this is more about the newspaper."

"It's only about the newspaper because we're publishing the stories that you guys keep secret," Chastity said.
"Why do you think it's been so easy for me to hire away
your agents?"

Blythe began ticking reasons off on her fingers. "Better
hours. Flexibility in choosing assignments. Press-pass
access to concerts, shows and sporting events. The chance
to see their names in print. Great dance parties."

"You could have great dance parties too if you'd hire
Marcus to give the men a few lessons," Chastity retorted.
"All of the free beer in the world isn't going to teach

anybody how to tango. And it's our reporters who are getting kidnapped and held hostage all the time, not your agents."

"That's because we train our agents to avoid needlessly dangerous situations," Blythe pointed out. "Clive and I went through the records and none of your kidnapped reporters were former agents who went through our training camp."

"And that's one of the things we're all here to discuss," Clive said. "But first, we need to talk about the president's visit. He's planning to conduct sensitive negotiations with alien diplomats and I hope the press will show restraint in covering his activities until he's ready to announce the results."

"But the president is a public figure," Walter protested. "The Grenouthians keep track of the comings and goings of diplomats on all of the stations as part of their shipping news so they'll spot him immediately. If we pretend nothing's happening while the bunnies are reporting that the president of EarthCent is on Union Station looking for handouts, we'll have missed the opportunity to put a positive spin on the trip."

"I didn't think of that," Clive admitted, turning towards Blythe.

"He's right," Blythe said. "I'll warn Kelly."

"So why is Tinka here?" Lynx asked with her typical bluntness. "I mean, the Galactic Free Press has already stolen so many EarthCent Intelligence agents that we've practically merged, but are we going to start integrating InstaSitter now?"

"Tinka is here to talk about our scholarship program," Chastity replied. "She'll do a brief presentation and then we'll explain why it matters. Tinka?"

The young Drazen woman, who had effectively been running day-to-day operations at InstaSitter since Chastity left to start the Galactic Free Press, rose from her seat. She glanced at her tab, tapped the corner of the screen, and the wall of the conference room behind her lit up with a densely packed bar graph.

"These are the basic InstaSitter financials as prepared by our CFO, Stanley Doogal, who couldn't be here today," Tinka began. "The girls told me to share everything, so you should know that I'm a ten-percent stakeholder in InstaSitter. Please don't let that information leave this room or my parents will get buried in proposals from all the wrong suitors. As far as the Drazen community knows, I just have a symbolic share."

"Is ten percent a lot?" Lynx asked.

"Let's just run through the numbers and you'll see," Tinka replied, sounding rather like Libby during one of her presentations. "InstaSitter is now active on seventy-one Stryx stations, many of which have larger populations than the hundred-million-odd sentients who live here. In all of the locations where we operate, the station librarian handles our reservations and back-office work for a percentage of the gross. That leaves our management free to focus on the hiring, training and retention of quality babysitters. Although the adolescent girls of some species have begun imitating the human tradition of offering paid babysitting services to neighbors, we have one-hundred-percent market share as the only commercial provider of on-call babysitters for every species living on the stations."

"Is that graph with all the station names showing your annual profits?" Lynx asked. "It looks like you're making hundreds of thousands of creds on every station."

26

"It's totaled at the bottom," Woojin said. "Just over twenty million."

"That's not our profit," Tinka informed them. "It's the number of InstaSitters we employ."

Lynx felt her jaw drop and swallowed. "You employ over twenty million people?"

"We employ over twenty million sentients of all species, including artificials," Tinka corrected her. "The majority of them are part-timers, and just over a quarter-million are Humans. Working for InstaSitter has become a rite-of-passage for the young females of some species."

"Wait a second, let me do the math," Woojin said. "If your sitters average one gig a week, say, five hours, that's about a hundred million billable hours a week, or five billion hours of babysitting a year."

"The average is closer to ten hours a week," Tinka informed him. "Some of the sitters work full-time or more, especially the artificials."

"How much do you net on an hour of babysitting?" Lynx asked, her voice sounding strangely hoarse.

"After the Stryx cut, we target around one cred per assignment, say, two-hundred millicreds an hour. Ninety percent of our gross goes to the sitters in pay and benefits. It's why nobody has bothered trying to compete with us on a commercial scale."

Woojin whistled. "So you're hauling in over a billion creds a year. I guessed you were millionaires, but I was off by a factor of a thousand."

"It just turned out that way," Blythe said, reentering the discussion. "We got this far by ethically employing a lot of kids, many of them the same age as the so-called 'clients' the new labor agencies are recruiting. Let's see the scholarship numbers, Tinka."

"When the girls first asked me to set up a scholarship program a few years ago, I didn't understand what they were talking about," the Drazen girl continued. "But students of all species are happy to have a little extra spending money, so we provide a stipend to sitters who show financial need while studying. Humans end up being the main beneficiaries, so I'll just show those results."

"Why are humans the big winners if we're barely over two percent of InstaSitter's workforce?" Lynx asked.

"The rest of us solved our student financing issues a long time ago," Tinka explained. "Education is the best investment a species can make in its future. But the interesting thing is where your sitters are spending their scholarships."

"It's just a list of Stryx stations," Woojin commented as he skimmed through the names and amounts. "Oh, there are some alien worlds at the bottom."

"Nobody goes back to Earth?" Lynx asked.

"There it is, between a Verlock academy world and a Frunge factory that takes student trainees," Woojin said. "Is there any detail beyond the stipend amount?"

Tinka selected the sum displayed for the Earth listing and a breakdown appeared.

"Three music students, a Russian literature major and a chef?"

"Practically all of the InstaSitter alumni end up studying in the Stryx Open University system, which is why the stations dominate the list," Tinka explained. "The five InstaSitters currently studying on Earth represent the highest number we've seen to date."

"Blythe and I both think that we're approaching an important turning point for people living away from Earth,"

Chastity said, taking over from Tinka. "New labor agencies owned by humans are rushing into the vacuum created by expiring alien contracts and counting on an affinity pitch to sign up workers. They use bonuses to tempt young people to go directly into the unskilled labor market, rather than pursuing an education or vocational training."

Clive picked up where his sister-in-law left off. "I didn't understand the importance of the Galactic Free Press stories on the labor market until Blythe and Chas sat me down and explained them. Given the numbers involved, I see a danger that a few unregulated contracting agencies will become a sort of default government for humans. And it's in their best interest to maximize the number of humans working as low-skilled laborers, because workers with advanced skills can find jobs on their own."

"Does EarthCent have a policy position on this yet?" Walter asked.

"If these new labor agencies were recruiting on Earth we could regulate them, but since they're strictly focused on workers coming off of expiring alien contracts, they're operating out of our jurisdiction," Clive replied. "We think the best solution is to offer young people a viable option by rebuilding the educational and industrial infrastructure on Earth to provide them with marketable skills."

"Which is why I hoped Jeeves would sneak in," Blythe said. "He's our expert on how the Stryx will react."

"I thought he was their expert on how humans react," Walter objected.

"Six of this, half-dozen of the other," Blythe replied with a shrug. "He got Daniel promoted, didn't he?"

"I'm still trying to understand that one," Walter admitted. "Why would the Stryx wait for Daniel to print new business cards before offering him a promotion?"

"The Stryx have always respected actions over words," Chastity said. "It's the same reason they won't put in a tunnel connection to a new world until they see enough of an investment in money or people. If EarthCent can convince human expatriates to return to Earth for training, I'm confident the Stryx will work with us on the transportation costs."

"Alright, let's move on to the kidnapping issue," Clive said. "The Galactic Free Press hired EarthCent Intelligence to look into the reasons the number of kidnappings has been growing faster than the number of active correspondents. While it's always possible that the Grenouthians are involved, my gut feeling is that it comes down to insufficient training for reporters and poor supervision on the part of the editorial staff."

"Tell us what you really think," Walter said sourly.

"I just did," Clive replied, ignoring the sarcasm in the managing editor's voice. "To be fair, your stories prove that you've taught your correspondents how to investigate tips and report the relevant facts. My contention is that the paper has gotten caught up in competing with the Grenouthians. You're sending people into situations they're unequipped to deal with, especially since they don't have the backing of the bunny networks. Do your subscribers really need daily updates about the pirates who lurk around the edges of the tunnel network?"

"Clive's got a point," Chastity interjected, before her mercurial managing editor could object. "We got into this business to provide an alternative to the sensationalism peddled by the Grenouthians. Some of our correspondents have displayed extraordinarily bad sense when it comes to putting themselves at risk."

"Is it finally my turn to speak?" Thomas asked. "We're currently losing a third of each new class of EarthCent Intelligence agents to the Galactic Free Press within two years of graduation. I suggested to Blythe that we could reduce the demand if we offer to train reporters for the paper. Our regular staff will teach situational awareness and use role-playing to walk the reporters through some of the dangerous scenarios they may encounter in the field. The paper will provide somebody to train the younger reporters in what constitutes a reasonable journalistic risk."

"How long would you need them for?" Walter asked.

"A week would be ideal, in part because we could fit a few classes in between our regularly scheduled training camps for new intelligence hires. We would give them an hour of self-defense training to start each morning, but other than teaching them the best spots to kick the various aliens, the main purpose of hand-to-hand combat exercises is to get them to take us seriously. The real goal of the course will be teaching them how to avoid getting into a situation where they need to remember where to kick an alien."

"I have to admit that sounds reasonable," Walter said. "How many reporters can you handle at a time?"

"I suggest we start with a dozen or so, and if it works well, we can always ramp up."

"And we won't need to retrain any of the staff we swiped from my sister," Chastity added.

"As long as we're all laying our cards on the table, how many subscribers does the paper have?" Lynx asked suddenly.

31

"We're over seven million paid subscribers, and closing on three hundred million unpaid," Chastity replied. "The cost to paid subscribers varies with whether they take the whole paper or just their regional news."

"I didn't know there was a free version," Thomas said. "What am I getting in the paid version that I'll lose?"

"You actually get more with the free version," Chastity replied with a grin. "Assuming you like reading advertisements, that is."

"Let me make sure I have everything straight," Lynx said. "You think that if Earth can't provide the children of contract laborers a way to move up the ladder, the people running the labor agencies will end up becoming the kings of humanity?"

"Look at the Dollnicks," Clive said. "Their entire society is structured around the wealth of their merchant princes. I'm not saying it can't work, but the Dollys have had a couple million years to establish networks of family retainers and work out the kinks. And their wealth is based on their engineering accomplishments, primarily terraforming new worlds."

"Have you been reading the stories in the paper?" Chastity asked Lynx. "The contracts these new agencies are pushing make me ashamed to be human. The only thing keeping them from turning vulnerable people into virtual slaves is that the aliens have higher standards than we do."

"You mean the human labor agencies are offering human workers worse conditions than the original contracts their parents signed back on Earth?" Lynx asked.

"That's exactly what I mean. Although much of the compensation was deferred until contract completion in the Stryx-approved agreements, the employer had to supply all necessities. Not just food, clothing and shelter, but medical services, teacher bots for children, a defined workweek and vacation days."

"The new contracts don't cover that stuff?"

"You have to read the fine print," Chastity said. "Millions of young people signed a contract with the GoHuman agency that would have obligated them to buy their own food, clothes and rent living space at fixed prices from the employer. The agency worded the contract so it looked like they were listing the value of benefits, but in fact, it was an agreement to purchase. We ran the calculations and it turned out that the average worker would have gone into debt before the two-year term was up."

"So what happened?"

"GoHuman couldn't find any aliens willing to accept workers under those conditions. Then word got out and the management disappeared."

"You know, I spent ten years as an independent trader before I got recruited by EarthCent Intelligence and I used to get mad about all the aliens I met looking down on us," Lynx said. "Now I'm beginning to wonder if they were right. What kind of galaxy is it when alien businessmen treat humans better than we treat each other?"

"There's a reason we call them advanced species," Chastity said without irony. "Putting aside technology, the aliens we know have all had ample time to work out stable systems. Some of their solutions are plain weird, like the Vergallian tech-ban worlds where they run a feudal society backed by a space fleet, but none of them are looking for shortcuts. When the Dollnicks invest trillions of creds in terraforming a new world, it's because they've long since worked out the economics and they know that it's good business."

"Wouldn't it be better business if they got the laborers cheaper?" Walter asked.

"The cost of the human laborers on a terraforming project is a minor part of the equation compared to all of the other factors involved," Chastity explained. "The last thing the Dollnicks want is problems with the labor force. They're willing to pay a fair wage, the same as the Drazens who employ humans for mining and factory work, or any of the other species who hire us."

"I still don't understand why they don't use robots," Walter said.

"That's because you refuse to take the time to go through Libbyland," Chastity told him. "The advanced species, the stable ones, have all learned that automation is ultimately a work-killer, and without work, biologicals atrophy. If they can't hire cheap biological labor, most species will use mechanicals sparingly for planting and harvesting, but that's pretty much it."

"And the artificial people from various species handle a lot of the Zero-G mass-manufacturing that does use automation," Thomas pointed out. "On the tunnel network, since the Stryx recognize AI as sentients with the right to self-determination, most of the advanced species have long since given up creating artificial people, except as research projects. That's why there just aren't that many of us."

"Alright, we've gone way off topic here," Clive said, rising from the table. "Thomas will be point on training the reporters, Woojin and Lynx will be assigned to the president for his stay to provide any support he requests, and Walter will coordinate press coverage for the presidential visit."

"What are you going to be doing?" Lynx asked.

"I'll be working with Blythe and Daniel behind the scenes to try to line up alien manufacturers willing to talk to the president," Clive replied. "I hope he's a good salesman, because when it comes right down to it, I have a hard time seeing what Earth has to offer them in return."

# Four

"I know I promised I'd stop, but this one is driving me nuts," Kelly said. "What's a five letter word for 'poor man's chocolate' with an 'r' in the middle?"

"Carob," Donna replied. "How can you not know that? Aisha and I both bake with it all of the time and you eat half of what we make. The Hadads always let us know whenever a new shipment of carob comes into the Shuk."

"I brought in carob cookies that Shaina made three days ago," Daniel reminded the ambassador. "You ate them all while I was scouting locations for the presidential reception."

"Oh, right. I was trying to think of a cheap kind of real chocolate. Maybe I'm not cut out to do crossword puzzles."

"Let's just concentrate on preparing for the president's visit," Donna said. "How long will he be on the station?"

"He left it open, depending on how the meetings with alien diplomats and businessmen go. If he can find serious negotiation partners, he said he'll stay here as long as it takes. Libby told me that the Stryx will foot the bill for all of his travel arrangements, but the president sort of invited himself to stay with me at home."

"I checked with the Empire Convention Center, and all of their high-end reception rooms are booked through the end of the cycle," Donna said. "Your office is barely big enough for the president to meet with aliens one-on-one, if they're even willing to come to him. We may be stuck holding the reception in Mac's Bones after all."

"Other than our friends, do you think any of the aliens will actually agree to meet the president?" Kelly asked. After two decades on the station, she was acutely aware that most alien relations with humans were driven by temporary shared interests, rather than a desire to accept EarthCent as an equal partner.

"They'll show up as a professional courtesy because they owe you," Donna said. "You go to every embassy reception the aliens hold when some big wheel from back home comes to visit. We've never held a first-class reception before, though some of the parties in Mac's Bones were pretty successful. The trick will be getting them to stay for more than a few minutes. Do you think a ball would work?"

"You're a genius! Ball. A four letter word for 'raw crumbles' that starts with a 'b' and has an 'l' in the third place. I missed the cookie connection."

"What?" Daniel asked.

"Before the cookie crumbles, it has to get baked, and before it's baked, you make a sort of a ball from raw dough."

"This is exactly why I don't do crossword puzzles," Donna commented. "What did you say the title of this one is?"

"Baker's History," Kelly replied. "That's why it's all about ingredients or prep work. I'll tell you what. I'll pay for lunch today, and if I can get Aisha and Laurel to meet us, I'm sure we could get through this puzzle before Dring brings me his solution."

37

"It's your turn to buy Friday lunch anyway," Donna pointed out. "I'll play along if you can explain why you've become so obsessed over these puzzles."

"I don't know. They seem to get stuck inside my head somehow."

"It's because you keep trying to solve them on your heads-up display," Donna said in exasperation. "Didn't you tell me that Dring does them on paper?"

"Parchment. He draws the whole thing, but that's because he's an artist. I once tried recreating the puzzle on the back of a pizza box but it came out a mess."

"I'll start printing them for you on immunization certificates," Donna offered. "We still have boxes of those to use up and you can get pencils from EarthCent Intelligence. Now, can we get back to work?"

"Sorry. Uh, you were suggesting a fancy-dress dance?"

"Not a dance, a ball. With a live orchestra and somebody in a uniform to announce the guests. Do you think Woojin would do it?"

"Wait. What? You want us to hold a ball like in fairy tales?"

"Balls used to be a big part of the diplomatic world, at least in Old Europe."

"We don't have time to bring in a human orchestra so we'd have to hire Vergallians," Kelly said. "I'm not saying people wouldn't enjoy it, but considering the Empire of a Hundred Worlds was getting ready to add us to their 'conquered' list before the Stryx stepped in, it would send the wrong message for the first visit of the president."

"I guess you're right," Donna allowed, putting aside her secret dream of organizing the ultimate diplomatic event. "It wouldn't be the same with recorded music. But if you want the alien diplomats to stay for longer than it takes to

38

meet the president and say something offensive about our lack of progress, we'll need more than colorful decorations."

"Jeeves just pinged me and we now have permission to use the medieval castle he and Paul have been working on for Libbyland," Daniel said, rejoining the conversation. "There are a lot of details to be worked out, but you know how many aliens are obsessed with old-fashioned weapons and armor."

"That's a great idea, but don't let it distract you from catering arrangements," Donna said.

"I was going to ask you to handle that part," Daniel admitted. "The main problem with the castle is that they haven't hired any staff yet and we only have a week to get ready. They're using holograms to make the most of the deck clearance, so the castle looks like it's built on a rocky mountain, with a single approach road. The wall facing the road is wide enough for a couple hundred guests if there aren't any defenders taking up space, but the interior rooms and the great hall won't be finished in time. They eventually plan to have reenactors attacking the castle, but Paul says there's room to stage a battle out front if I can line up the actors."

"Maybe Bork knows somebody who can help," Kelly suggested. "You know he uses all of his vacation time doing background acting work for immersives."

"Isn't the medieval castle supposed to be on Earth?" Donna asked. "You'll have to remind me which country had the knights with the tentacles."

"I remember him saying that on-station auditions are really competitive, so there must be a lot of reenactors around," Kelly said, warming to her own idea. "I'll stop by the Drazen embassy tomorrow and ask Bork if he knows anybody."

Strains of the EarthCent anthem penetrated the office and the ambassador and the embassy manager exchanged a puzzled look.

"Daniel? Are you angling for another promotion already?" Kelly asked.

"Always," Daniel replied. "Shaina says that ambition in a husband is a turn-on, but what does that have to do with the awful music?"

"I know," Donna said ruefully. "Every year when I fill in EarthCent's employee feedback form, I always tell them to lose the anthem and get something that a normal person can sing. Where is the music coming from, Libby?"

"If you'll direct your attention to the entrance," the Stryx librarian replied. The door slid open and a familiar woman stepped into the opening.

"Hildy?" It had been a couple of years since Kelly had last seen EarthCent's public relations director, but strangely enough, the woman looked younger than she remembered.

"Do I really have to do this?" Hildy asked, looking back over her shoulder into the corridor. She sighed, and then put on the brightest smile she could muster and announced, "Ladies and Gentlemen. I give you the President of EarthCent."

The irritating anthem swelled to a crescendo, and Stephen Beyer strode into the embassy, looking a bit sheepish about his grand entry. "Thank you, Librarian," he shouted over the loud whooshing noise that the composer had intended to represent the fleets of alien transports landing on Earth. The anthem cut off abruptly.

"What are you doing here?" Kelly exclaimed, jumping up from her seat. "You aren't supposed to arrive for another week."

"We decided to turn it into a sort of a honeymoon," the president replied happily. "You know Hildy Greuen."

"But aren't you already, er..." Kelly cut herself off before the "M" word escaped.

"Sort of," Stephen replied. "That's why it's only sort of a honeymoon. But I've been separated from my wife for years now, if that makes you feel more comfortable."

"Oh, I'm sorry. About your separation I mean, I didn't know. Not that there's anything wrong with you, Hildy. Oh, that didn't come out right. No offense."

"None taken," the president's companion said. "I'm going to have to get used to being a home-wrecker, so what better place to start than with friends?"

"You're not a home-wrecker," Stephen said in irritation. He put his arm around her waist and addressed the embassy staff. "After all those years living on Stryx stations, my wife couldn't stand being back on Earth. I always hated living on stations myself, and our kids were all grown, so we decided to try living apart for a while. Then she took up with—it's not important, but I promised not to divorce her until she was ready to settle down."

"Settle down?" Kelly said. "I'm afraid I don't get it."

"One of the few perks of the EarthCent presidency is that the Stryx pay all travel expenses for the president and spouse," Stephen informed them. "I suspect when they established that policy they didn't have this situation in mind, but my wife loves to travel, and she made some kind of bargain with them that I don't even want to know about."

"Well, let's get the two of you settled in," Kelly offered. "I haven't prepared your rooms, uh, or room yet, but you must be tired from the trip."

"We spent all three days in stasis so we're well rested," the president said. "I always hated Zero-G. In any case, we reserved a hotel room for the first week, that's the honeymoon part. I'm not officially here for another six days and seventeen hours."

"And why are you here now, Mr. President?" Daniel asked politely.

"Excellent question, Consul Cohan. I was waiting for somebody to ask. Last month, my office sponsored a convention for the heads of companies from all over Earth. A few of them are doing well making playing cards and kitchen gadgets, and ever since the orbital elevators were built, the food companies have been raking it in providing supplemental supplies for human laborers all over the tunnel network. But our technology companies have been transformed into importers for cheap alien products."

"We've been planning a campaign to promote Earth's higher education system to the children of expatriate laborers, which is why your criticisms of our universities struck such a chord," Hildy added. "We think it's of vital importance to get some of the best and brightest of humanity reconnected with Earth, even if it's initially just for a few years of education."

"But what can you offer them?" Kelly asked. "I'm sure that Earth is a fine place to study human history or literature, but for most career paths, students are better off with the Open University on the stations, or getting on-the-job training from alien employers that accept them in apprenticeship programs."

"We're aware of that, and we're also aware that many young humans who would have pursued a higher education one or two generations ago are instead settling on open worlds or becoming small traders," the president said. "Our concern is that we are on the brink of completely losing our educational infrastructure and that future generations will come to accept our technological inferiority as the status quo. We have the beginnings of a plan to address this, and rather than sitting around Earth talking it to death, I decided to visit Union Station and put it to the test."

"What test is that, sir?" Daniel asked.

"Welcoming an alien invasion," the president replied. "Regular contact with alien diplomats is the one thing I miss about being an ambassador. The only aliens I see on Earth are either tourists who come slumming or shady businessmen hoping to sell us obsolete weapons systems. It may sound strange to you, but if I want to find out what the other species are thinking, I have to ask the station ambassadors to do the talking for me."

"So you want to approach the other species about re-building Earth's education system?" Kelly asked doubtfully.

"I want to invite them to open campuses on Earth," the president said. "It's the only way my people could think of to get around the existing education cartel. I'm sure it's easy for you to forget when you're living out here, but the old national governments on Earth still exist, primarily as pay-for-service entities. They usually keep a low profile because they don't want to push more people into emigrating and losing what's left of their fee base but they're still deeply entrenched in the education system."

"That's an interesting idea," Donna said. "If I remember the EarthCent charter correctly, the president can award alien holdings with exterritorial status, like an embassy, so that the national governments wouldn't have jurisdiction. If an alien school starts attracting the best students, the existing universities will have no choice but to adapt or shut down."

"Exactly. And we're also hoping that alien-run facilities will be more attractive to the children of expatriate laborers," the president said. "We've all seen how humans living on open worlds come to identify with the host species, and the same is true for most contract laborers. When it comes to kids who grew up on the Drazen or Dollnick worlds where their parents are working, we'll have a much better chance of attracting them to study on Earth if the Drazens and Dollnicks are running the programs."

"It might just work," Kelly said. "I'm sure I can get you a meeting with the Drazen ambassador any time, and the Dollnick ambassador will probably agree to talk since there's a potential profit involved."

"Let's wait until after my official reception," the president told her. "I was serious about this week being our sort-of honeymoon, but sneaking onto the station and running around behind your back would have been rude. Besides, I'm told the Grenouthians keep tabs on the movements of alien diplomats, even lowly humans."

"But why should the aliens agree to help?" Daniel asked. "What advantage do they gain by educating humans to compete with them? Whatever money they might earn from running extension campuses would surely be trivial compared to what they could lose if humans start manufacturing goods that can compete with their own products."

"We don't think it will be much of an issue," Hildy said. "For one thing, the advanced species view us as so backwards and they outnumber us so greatly that it would be hard for them to see us as a threat."

"Just look at how many of the aliens we're familiar with spend their time terraforming and colonizing new worlds, or who introduce tech-bans on highly populated planets," the president pointed out. "High-tech is never going to employ the majority of our population, but if we don't get on the bus we're liable to find ourselves under it."

"What?" the three embassy employees asked at the same time.

"It's marketing talk, from Earth," Hildy explained. "I've been preparing him to make a sales pitch to the aliens. We've been doing our homework on how alien economies work, and we were surprised to learn that domestic production and consumption accounts for over ninety percent of their activity."

"But they trade all of the time," Daniel objected. "Trade is what the tunnel network is all about, and every species has its specialties."

"And this is where living on a Stryx station colors the way you see things," the president lectured the young diplomat. "The vast majority of the alien populations live on worlds, not in space. Even with orbital elevators, the cost of shipping means that it's mainly specialty goods that get imported and exported. There are exceptions, of course, like mining worlds that bring in a lot of food as an alternative to synthesizing everything, but for the main part, settled worlds end up producing most of what they need locally. In fact, there's little point in settling a world that doesn't have the capacity to sustain its population."

"For example, we think the Frunge could open a factory on Earth manufacturing machine tools for humans," Hildy said. "We'd ask for technology transfer in return for giving them an exclusive deal, but they don't have to worry much about humans making merchandise that will compete with factories on their worlds. The freight cost would offset any advantage we would have on labor, and that doesn't even take into account understanding the market, branding, supply channels, and customer relations."

"So what exactly is the goal on attracting alien industries to Earth?" Daniel asked.

"Knowledge," the president answered in one word. "Humans working in a Frunge factory will learn something of their techniques, and hopefully, the management will come to respect our capabilities. The Stryx gave us a great gift in opening Earth, but in at least one sense, they also saddled us with a handicap. We never went through the formative experience of developing interstellar travel on our own, yet it would be crazy for us to ignore alien technology at this point. We have to play catch-up, and that means learning what we can from the other species rather than sticking our heads in the sand."

"You make it sound like there are people who hold a different view," Kelly said.

"That's putting it mildly. There are a number of reasons to remain on Earth, of course, but I wouldn't be going out on a limb to say that a good proportion of the people back home are basically alien rejectionists."

"They don't accept that aliens exist?" Daniel asked.

"There are some of those as well, though they're more of a fringe element," the president replied. "Large numbers

46

of people believe that the aliens are a threat to our natural development, whatever that means, and that anything not invented by humans on Earth is bad for us by definition."

"Unfortunately, these attitudes are particularly strong wherever there are vested interests who see potential alien involvement in Earth affairs as a threat to their status," Hildy said.

"Like in higher education," Kelly guessed.

"Exactly," the president confirmed. "Hildy researched that issue as well, and it turns out that arguments about tenure and the overhead costs of school administrations have been going on for over a century. I believe that our ability to recontextualize globally will allow us to effectivize dynamically."

"What?" the three embassy employees asked.

"I've created a marketing monster," Hildy groaned.

# Five

Dorothy sat on the corner of a ratty couch which was covered with a Vergallian horse blanket, wishing that she had gone to Pub Haggis to wait for the end of David's shift rather than telling him to meet her at the party. She felt horribly overdressed in the crowd of alien hippies and she wasn't used to wearing the high heels that Chance had pushed on her. Even worse, the artificial person hadn't shown up yet, and Dorothy was beginning to wonder if her impulsive friend had gotten sidetracked by something more interesting.

"Want to dance?" a copper-colored Horten boy asked her abruptly.

"I'm just waiting for my boyfriend," Dorothy replied with a polite smile. She'd never seen a copper Horten before, and though she suspected it might be a compliment, she decided she'd rather not know.

"Dorothy? What are you doing here?" asked a Drazen woman, plopping down beside the girl on the couch.

"Tinka!" Dorothy's face lit up with pleasure and relief. "Did you just come in? I thought I didn't know anybody, and a human in this place sticks out like a sore thumb."

"I'm here on an arranged date," Tinka said. "He's waiting for his turn on stage. Where's your boyfriend?"

"He's cooking tonight, but they must be having a late rush because he should have been here by now." Dorothy lowered her voice and leaned closer to the Drazen. "I hope your date is a better singer than that Fillinduck trio. I don't get how anybody can dance to that music."

"If you call it music, or dancing for that matter," Tinka said. "My date won't be singing though. He's a poet."

"Oh. I'm sorry."

"Yeah. My mother's second cousin sings in a chorus with a friend of his brother's meditation tutor. Sometimes I wonder if I should just let my mother hire a professional matchmaker, but I thought if I asked them to stick with informal introductions there would be a better chance of getting dates with guys I know."

"Don't you have any say in the matter?"

"I get final say if the guy proposes, but it's traditional for the families to line up candidates and handle the contract negotiations when it gets serious."

"Drazens have marriage contracts too? I just found out that Frunge have contracts a couple weeks ago."

"All of the species have marriage contracts, except you guys," Tinka said. "I was shocked when Blythe married Clive without even establishing a pre-marital asset-holding structure for her InstaSitter share, though I guess that Effterii ship of his is worth quite a bit as well. But I know they didn't stipulate the number of children she would bear or any of the important stuff. And then when Chas got married, the only thing her husband brought to the partnership was his wardrobe."

"He's pretty nice," Dorothy said. "My brother has been taking dance lessons with him for two years now. Blythe says that she's going to enter Samuel and Vivian in the next Vergallian Junior's competition if she can get my mother to go along with it."

"Uh oh. I'm afraid my date is about to start."

49

There was a polite round of applause as the Fillinduck trio stepped down from the small stage, which was really just a few sturdy folding tables with their legs clamped together to keep them stable. A Drazen male with a string of beads wrapped around his tentacle carefully ascended the improvised stairs, stepping from a small box, onto the seat of a chair, and then onto a table-top. There was a flurry of movement as some of the dancers sought seats and the more knowledgeable party-goers decided to see what was going on in the other rooms. A Vergallian couple wedged onto the couch next to Tinka.

"So, hello," the Drazen poet said. "I'm Jord, and I'd like to give you a Dinge I've been working on about the station."

"What's a Dinge?" Dorothy whispered to Tinka. "It didn't translate."

"It's one of the traditional forms of poetry males do," Tinka whispered back. "No structure, no meter, no rhyme or rhythm."

On the stage, the Drazen cleared his throat and began striking and holding a series of poses that reminded Dorothy of the warm-up exercises Woojin did before teaching unarmed combat.

"Is he working up the courage to start?" Dorothy whispered after several minutes of almost painful silence.

"No, he's doing it now," Tinka replied. "Did I forget to mention, no words?"

Suddenly, the poet knelt with a dramatic thud, and reaching down with his tentacle behind his back, pulled one of his ankles up until it projected over his shoulder. His body trembled with the strain, and Dorothy heard a sharp "pop." Several of the Drazens lounging about whistled. Then it was over, and he limped off the stage. A

50

Horten band immediately began deploying their equipment on the tables as the poet made his way to the couch.

"What did you think?" Jord asked, eyeing Tinka hopefully.

"That was truly painful," the Drazen woman said, though the translation the human girl got through her implant gave the words a strangely complimentary intonation. "Dorothy. Please meet Jord."

"It was really interesting," Dorothy said, exchanging a limp handshake with the poet. Out of the corner of her eye, she saw Tinka cringe.

"Interesting?" Jord repeated, looking like he'd been slapped across the face.

"I meant, uh, boring," Dorothy stuttered, looking to the Drazen woman for confirmation. Tinka shook her head in the negative and pulled her tentacle over her mouth. "I meant, it's a new human expression, you know?" the girl tried desperately. "When something is, like, really painful, we say it's interesting and boring."

"Thank you," Jord said, regaining his composure. "I was afraid you detected some structure in the movements that I'd failed to eliminate."

"No, no," Dorothy protested vehemently. "Nothing but pain, start to finish."

The Drazen poet's chest swelled up and he couldn't suppress a broad smile of self-satisfaction. "Can I bring you ladies some drinks?" he offered.

Tinka nodded her head and mumbled the name of a drink without taking the tentacle away from her mouth, and Dorothy added, "Water, if you see any." Jord headed off to the bar.

"I almost died," Tinka exploded the instant the poet was out of earshot. "An interesting Dinge. That's the

51

funniest thing I've ever heard. I thought I'd bite through my tentacle to keep from laughing. Look, I really put teeth marks in it."

"I'm so sorry," Dorothy said. "My mother taught me that 'interesting' is the safest thing to say when you don't know what to make of alien art."

"It's not supposed to be art," Tinka said through her laughter. "The idea of Dinge is to be anti-art. I don't have a clue what the point is."

"Does that mean that Jord isn't your Mr. Right?" Dorothy ventured.

The young Drazen woman rolled her eyes. "A Dinge poet? Besides, didn't you see that thing on the side of his nose?"

"The little black spot?"

"It looks little now, but in a hundred years or so it will be the size of a five-cred piece. My father has one, so I should know."

"Couldn't he have it removed?"

"Drazens don't go in for that sort of thing," Tinka said. "I shouldn't complain, though, since the last guy my parents set me up with smelled completely wrong."

"Do you mean bad?"

"No, just wrong. Like you came home from work and found yourself in somebody else's apartment kind of wrong. You know."

"I guess," Dorothy said uncertainly.

"Hey." The Vergallian guy sitting next to Tinka exhaled a cloud of blue smoke and offered her a smoldering stick. "Kraaken Red, fresh off a trader."

"Thanks," Tinka said, carefully accepting the stick. She blew on the tip to freshen the ember, then waved a handful of smoke towards her nose and inhaled it before handing the stick back.

"None for your friend?" the Vergallian asked in wonder. "It's good stuff. I see humans do it all the time."

"She's younger than she looks and I know her mother," the Drazen replied, exhaling blue fumes.

"I've inhaled stuff," Dorothy protested.

"Yeah, like smoke from your father's barbeque," Tinka retorted. "I usually wouldn't do this myself, but I have to put in a full shift with Jord or it doesn't count."

"Count for what?"

"For an arranged date," Tinka replied, looking surprised that Dorothy didn't get it. "I have to go on six a year or I'll never hear the end of it. Hey, let me see your hand."

Dorothy held her hand up for the Drazen woman, who placed her own hand against it.

"I always feel funny about you guys missing a thumb," she continued, waggling her sixth digit to make the point. "I guess the Stryx don't get everything right after all."

"Tell me about it," said the Vergallian man, offering Tinka the Kraaken stick for another hit. "I'm afraid to go on a date without taking anti-pheromone pills."

"That's something the Stryx did get right," the Vergallian's gorgeous date said, leaning forward so she could wink at Dorothy. "Anyway, it's not incompatible with free will."

"Oh, no. Every time she inhales she gets like this," the Vergallian guy groaned.

"I didn't know Vergallians believed in free will," Dorothy said. "I heard you were all Higher Determinists, whatever that means."

"It means that if you believe you have free will, it doesn't matter that you really don't," Jord said, handing Dorothy a glass of water. "Mind if I have a sniff of that?"

Tinka exchanged the Kraaken stick for the mixed drink her date had brought and sat back, letting her head flop to face the human girl.

"It's like, if you have two choices, and you make one, does that mean you have free will?"

"I guess," Dorothy ventured. "I mean, there was a famous poet back on Earth who wrote that choosing one of two paths, even if they're practically the same, makes all the difference."

"But what if the choices aren't really free?" the stoned Vergallian girl asked, leaning forward again to make eye contact with Dorothy. "What if you have ten choices, or a hundred, but the results of every single option converge on some predetermined path?"

"But how could anybody know?" Dorothy protested. "The number of possible futures that come about because I did or didn't get to inhale any Kraaken Red must be approaching infinity after just a few days."

"Approaching infinity?" Jord repeated. "Don't you guys study Convergence Theory in school?"

"We didn't have that," Dorothy admitted. "What is it? A kind of math?"

"Convergence Theory is the basis of Higher Determinism," the Vergallian girl said. She put her elbow on one knee so she could hold her head up while leaning forward to see Dorothy. The muscle relaxant component in the Kraaken Red was taking effect on all of them, and Jord sat down cross-legged on the floor.

"We need a Verlock to explain it to her," the Vergallian male said, lurching unsteadily to his feet. "I'll go find one."

"I can explain it," his date said, pulling him back down. "She doesn't need a formal proof. It just means that most paths don't matter because they converge again anyway. Think about if you pricked your finger with a pin. Does it really matter whether the point sticks in a hair to one side or the other? If you make the pin infinitely sharp, there are an infinite number of places you can prick your finger, and which one you choose doesn't make a damn difference to the universe."

"Right on," Jord said, staring at his fingertips. Tinka nudged Dorothy and giggled.

"But most choices aren't about moving a pinprick this way or that way on a fingertip," the human girl protested.

"Really?" The Vergallian girl coughed out a cloud of blue smoke. "How about to a—what do you call those little insects they say outnumber people on Earth?"

"Ants," Dorothy replied. "Or maybe beetles."

"What difference does it make whether one of your ants is having a bad day, or whether you step on a hundred of them without knowing it? Do they still have free will because they follow their own paths?"

"Actually, I think I saw in a Grenouthian nature documentary that they follow pheromone trails too," the Vergallian man said ruefully.

"Whatever," the beautiful Vergallian girl continued. "The point is, if the powers-that-be want you to end up somewhere, that's where you end up. It doesn't matter how many choices you make with your free will along the way because all of the paths converge."

"Right on," Jord repeated.

"But sentients aren't at all like ants," Dorothy said. "Unless, did you mean that we're the ants and the Stryx...?"

The Vergallian held the fingers of the hand that wasn't supporting her head up to her lips and made a twisting motion. Then she sank back into the couch and began to snore loudly.

"Can't handle the Kraaken stick," her date commented. "She's a pretty good abstract sculptor though, and a great dancer."

"Hey," David said, looming over the sofa from the side. "I've been looking all over for you."

"I'm right here," Dorothy replied, taking a sip from her glass of water. She felt a little light-headed, and she wondered how much second-hand smoke she'd been inhaling.

The Horten band finally completed setting up all of their gear and the lead keyboard player unleashed a torrent of notes. David began bobbing his head with the bass sound of a giant tube that another of the colorful musicians was playing.

Dorothy fought the urge to put her hands over her ears and stood up, which caused Tinka to slowly list over to her right. The Drazen woman picked up her legs and ended up curled into the fetal position on her half of the couch. Jord looked disappointed, but he settled for turning around so he could sit facing the band with his head leaning back against his date's legs.

"We should find Chance," Dorothy shouted in David's ear. "She invited us, after all."

The tall boy shrugged and followed Dorothy into the next room of the Studio Club, a cooperative work and play space maintained by a group of artists and performers from various species. The bar area was packed solid, and everybody was shouting so loudly to be heard that it felt more like a racetrack than a party. David grabbed

Dorothy's hand and pulled her through an open doorway into a darker room with flashing lights.

The moment she crossed the threshold, Dorothy realized they had stepped through an acoustic barrier, because the overwhelming noise generated by the Horten band was replaced by the easily identifiable sound of Dollnick techno-music. Chance was at the center of a knot of leaping and gyrating dancers, lost in the hard-driving beat.

"At least it's not as loud," Dorothy said. "Want to dance?"

"I do my aerobics at work," David replied. "Were you inhaling back there? You shouldn't do that stuff."

"I was just sitting there," she protested, joining him against the wall. "Did you recognize Tinka?"

"That was Tinka? I've never seen her dressed down like that. When I was introduced to her at one of your picnics she looked like a rich Drazen business executive. Is she an artist?"

"She runs InstaSitter for Blythe and Chastity but she's here with her arranged date, who performed earlier. You're lucky you missed him." Dorothy turned to greet an alien youth. "Hey, Mornich. Long time no see."

The Horten's skin blurred through several color changes as he tried to place Dorothy. Finally he guessed, "The ambassador's daughter?"

"Dorothy. This is my boyfriend, David. So that band was too noisy even for a Horten, huh?"

"I'm the lead singer," the Horten ambassador's son replied stiffly. "It's traditional to leave the stage during opening instrumentals."

"About time you got here," Chance said, leaning around the Horten youth's shoulder.

"Where's Thomas?" Dorothy asked.

57

"He hates techno-music, he wouldn't come," the artificial person explained. "Do you dance?" she asked the Horten.

"I guess," Mornich said, somewhat overwhelmed by Chance's aggressive approach. "But I have to sing," he continued, pointing towards the other room.

"It can wait." Chance grabbed his extended arm and pulled him onto the dance floor.

"Don't even try it," David warned, as Dorothy gave his hand a tentative tug. "Hey, did you know that your brother and Jeeves are advertising for medieval cooks? Mrs. Ainsley says I should try out for it, but Ian acts like I'd be stabbing him in the back. I didn't know anything about cooking when you got me the job working for him."

"Never mind Ian," Dorothy said firmly. "You paid your dues washing dishes for two years and he's never said anything about making you a partner or leaving you Pub Haggis, has he? They have grown children of their own who they didn't want following them into the restaurant business so they must have had their reasons."

"I don't know if I'd want a job at Libbyland, though. The nice thing about working for the Ainsleys is that they're there all of the time, and they wouldn't ask me to do anything they wouldn't do themselves. When I worked for that mining outfit, I doubt the owner knew or cared how many kids were getting killed or crippled, or whether we got enough gravity time to stay healthy. We were all just numbers to them."

"Are you forgetting who owns Libbyland?" Dorothy asked. "You'd be working for Libby and she's there around the clock. The Stryx don't have to employ biologicals for anything, you know. They could do it all with bots."

"Well, maybe I'll look into it, but I still don't get why the station librarian runs a theme park."

"She makes money on it, especially the gift shop," Dorothy explained. "I'm not saying that's her main motivation, you never know with the Stryx. But they do use their own businesses, like renting space on the stations, to help keep the monetary system in balance. It's not for them. It's for the rest of us."

"And I thought that my date was boring," Tinka interrupted, putting a hand on Dorothy's shoulder for balance. "Is this really what Humans do on dates? Talk about monetary policy?"

"Where's Jord?" Dorothy asked.

"I woke up to some Horten percussionist screeching his head off like he'd never tried to sing before, and Jord said it was too painful to walk out on," the Drazen woman replied with a heavy sigh. "I think he knew if we came in here I'd expect him to move with the rhythm. Hey, who's that dancing with Chance?"

"Mornich, the Horten ambassador's son. He's the lead singer for the band."

"That explains a lot."

# Six

"Many of you are seeing each other for the first time, and you're probably wondering who's left out there getting the stories if you're all in here," Chastity said, speaking loudly to be heard over a dozen conversations. A sudden hush fell around the crowded newsroom and heads nodded in agreement. In addition to the thirty or so editors, rewrite specialists and layout artists who staffed the Galactic Free Press headquarters in shifts around the clock, two dozen correspondents were squeezed into the room, sitting on display desks and standing against the walls.

"The Grenouthians!" somebody called out from the back. There was a nervous laugh in response. A rumor was going around that the publisher wanted to cut headcount to save money and that the only question was whether the reporters in the room were the survivors or the road-kill. The smart money in the hastily arranged betting pool was on road-kill, since it didn't make sense to buy passage for correspondents from all over the galaxy just to tell them that they still had a job.

"In the last year, we've had to pay ransom to recover reporters in four separate incidents. Three of these were due to run-ins with pirates, which has led us to rethink our coverage of piracy between the frontiers of the tunnel network and the neighboring advanced species."

"But that's where the pirates gather," a woman's voice protested.

"Yes, and everybody knows that. What we're rethinking is whether it makes sense to cover piracy like it's some kind of sport, especially when ransoming three of the kidnapped correspondents back from pirates used up all of the money in this year's bonus pool."

The employees let out a collective sigh. A few correspondents were disappointed to hear that bonuses were out the window, but most of them were sighing from relief, since the publisher wouldn't be telling them this if they were fired.

"What about the fourth ransom?" another reporter asked.

"Our insurance paid that one since it was on a Vergallian world, but the local Thark bookmaker doesn't cover planets and volumes of space off the tunnel network. Four incidents in one year suggested to me that we've been doing something wrong, so I asked EarthCent Intelligence to assess our operations. Their conclusion," Chastity paused to theatrically brandish a tablet that she had borrowed from Tinka a few minutes earlier to use as a prop, "is that we are providing insufficient training for reporters entering danger zones, and that we should put you all through boot camp."

"John Daggert," a tough-looking man wearing a black uniform without any insignias spoke up. "I cover the Empire of a Hundred Worlds. Are you telling me that after a twenty-year stint in the mercenaries, I've got to go to boot camp with these kids to keep my job?"

"I'm aware of your background, John, and one of the recommendations from EarthCent Intelligence was to get you involved as an instructor, if you're willing. As it happens, the EarthCent Intelligence training facility is between classes, so we've scheduled a crash course for several of the lucky reporters in this room who were recalled for just that purpose."

"I've already been through Mac's Bones," a woman called out.

"Me too," chorused another voice from the back of the room.

"Everyone we hired away from EarthCent Intelligence gets a waiver. We didn't bring in so many of our senior foreign correspondents at the same time just to discuss ransom insurance and a change in editorial policy. The president of EarthCent is officially arriving on the station in two days and we want to show the Grenouthians and the rest of the galaxy that we take him seriously. Between training, reporting on the president, and meeting to come up with new coverage guidelines, I think we can keep you all busy for a couple of weeks."

"I thought Union Station was exclusively Steelforth's beat," a woman called out. The whole room dissolved in laughter as the young reporter turned bright red. The two most famous headlines in the history of the Galactic Free Press, 'EarthCent Ambassador Kelly McAllister Thinks Humans are Aliens,' and 'Alien Bites Dog,' had both appeared with Bob Steelforth's byline, even though they were penned by Walter.

"I'll take that as compliment to our city desk," Chastity said after the laughter died down. Just as the Galactic Free Press had adopted the archaic term "newspaper" to describe its business, the employees had fallen into randomly applying other newspaper terminology where it seemed to fit. Most of the lingo came from watching black-

and-white movies from the 1930's that were part of the orientation package for new employees.

"Speaking of the city desk," Walter said, rising and facing the crowded room, "while you're on the station, you'll be submitting your copy to the Union Station editor in addition to your regular editor. We'll decide on a case-by-case basis whether it makes more sense to add a story to local coverage of the president's visit, or to treat it as special correspondence for your regular beats. Many of our subscribers only pay for ad-free regional coverage, so if you believe a story fits in with an ongoing theme you've been developing, make sure to let us know."

"We've reserved Pub Haggis in the Little Apple to treat you all to lunch," Chastity announced. "That's still a good hour off, so I'm going to ask our Stryx librarian to ping the twenty of you we've registered for kidnapping school, that is, hostage avoidance training, and somebody will be available in Mac's Bones to explain the schedule and put you at ease. John, I wasn't kidding that we'd like to have you as an instructor while you're on the station, so please consider stopping by. Does anybody have any questions?"

"Katy Hicks. I cover the Dollnick ag worlds in the Echo Station sector."

"Yes, Katy?"

"I filed a story last month that got spiked and I want to know if that was a management decision or if somebody thought I was joking."

"Doesn't ring a bell," Chastity said, glancing around the room at her editorial staff. "Anybody?"

"Is this about the potato thing?" an irate voice asked.

"It's not a potato, it's a Dollnick Tan tuber," the reporter retorted. She reached in her shoulder bag and drew out a brown object, then made her way through the press of bodies to the front of the room. "What's the first thing that comes into your head?" she asked, handing it to Chastity.

The publisher of the Galactic Free Press looked at the tuber dubiously, turning it slowly, and then her jaw dropped. "It's Aisha," she declared.

"A human laborer on Dolag Twelve dug that up last month and it almost brought production to a halt. Their children all watch 'Let's Make Friends,' so they wanted to save it for a novelty, but the Dollnicks have a strict rule about laborers not holding anything back from non-terran crops. The workers took up a collection and bought it for a hundred creds, so this is the most expensive tuber you're ever likely to see."

"It does look just like Aisha," Walter agreed.

"So why do you have it here?" Chastity asked.

"I was in the area covering a story about a major contract expiration, but all anybody wanted to talk about was the tuber," Katy explained. "I wrote up the story with pictures, but it didn't run and I couldn't get an explanation why. The woman who dug up the tuber was so disappointed her picture wouldn't be in the paper that she let me have it to push for publication."

"It's a potato!" the irate voice repeated, and this time, the ag worlds editor got up from his desk and strode to the front. "Look, I worked with the Grenouthians for fifteen years before I signed on with the Free Press, and I swore to put all those 'Silly Humans' stories behind me. So somebody found a potato that looks a little —," he stopped and peered disdainfully at the Dollnick Tan, "a lot like Aisha McAllister, and it's supposed to be galactic news?"

"The laborers pooling their earnings to buy it from the Dollnick supervisor gives it a strong human interest angle," Walter said. "A hundred creds is a lot of money to people working a labor contract where the majority of the pay is deferred compensation."

The editor continued to stare at the tuber. "It really does look just like her," he said. "Did you take the picture from a bad angle or something?"

"The picture was perfect and I sent a half a dozen versions," Katy insisted. "I'll bet you glanced at the text and didn't even look at the images."

"Maybe so," the editor admitted. "I mean, what do you do with a thing like this? Even if humans could digest Dollnick Tans, who would eat it after seeing the face?"

"So you'll run the story?" Chastity asked.

"I'll go back and look at the copy," the editor said. The newsroom burst into applause. "You know, you should try to get it on her show for Surprise Day. My kids love that segment. I know the Grenouthian producer if you want me to ping him."

"That's what we need more of in the news business— happy endings," Chastity declared. "So I hope to see you all at Pub Haggis for lunch, and if there are any questions or complaints, please feel free to approach me at any time. And I was kidding about cancelling the bonuses. I just wanted to make sure I had your attention."

The newsroom broke into cheers, which spontaneously morphed into a rousing chorus of, "For she's a jolly good publisher," causing Chastity to blush for perhaps the second time in her adult life. She slipped out the exit and headed across the corridor to InstaSitter, where she returned her speaking prop to Tinka.

Two hours later, Joe and Paul found themselves unable to enter Pub Haggis through the front door because of the overflow crowd.

"Let's try around the kitchen side," Joe said. "I don't want to rupture somebody's Achilles tendon by running into the back of an ankle with the hand-truck."

"Why didn't he rent a delivery bot?" Paul asked. "I thought the Little Apple merchants had established a co-op that owned a whole stable of them."

"They're prone to sudden stops," Joe explained. "The bots are programmed to put the safety of station inhabitants first, so they can slosh the beer around pretty badly. Ian said he's never been caught so unprepared and he's going to need to tap these without giving them much time to settle. He's lucky I happened to have two kegs left from my last batch, and I'm lucky you came home for lunch or I'd have been stuck making two trips."

The kitchen door was open and Joe cautiously wheeled in the first keg, Paul following after him. Ian's wife, Torra, was so intent on the dozen or so orders she had going simultaneously on the grill that she didn't even turn her head as they came in. There were twice as many people as usual working in the modest-sized kitchen area, three of whom were wearing aprons that identified them as employees of nearby establishments. David was the first person to notice the beer delivery, and he called to his girlfriend's father, "Go straight through to the bar."

The swinging door between the kitchen and the dining room burst open as Joe approached, missing the leading edge of the keg by a hand's breadth. The bus boy barely avoided barreling into the keg, and it was fortunate he was using a tub rather than a tray, or his load of dirty dishes would have ended up on the floor. Somehow, Ian heard the sudden clatter of the dishes shifting in the plastic tub over the noisy conversations in the pub and stuck his head through the door.

"Just in time, boys," he cried in relief. "There's no room up here until I pull the empties. Hold on a minute." He withdrew his head and then reappeared two minutes later, an empty keg suspended by the rim in each beefy hand. "Take these," he said, handing the well-used aluminum kegs to Joe, who had already maneuvered the hand-truck out of the way of the swinging door, and stood it up so the bottom rested on the floor. Ian lifted the new keg easily, proving he hadn't finished second in the caber toss for lack of strength.

Joe turned to put down the empties and steeled himself to hoist the second keg, but Paul already had it aloft, a hand gripping each end. "I got it," he grunted. He carried the half-keg which weighed almost as much as he did close to his body, and followed Ian through the swinging door.

After moving the hand-trucks and the empty kegs back out of the kitchen, Joe joined Paul and Ian behind the bar. He was surprised to see Chance pulling pints for the customers and Thomas artfully juggling liquor bottles as he concocted mixed drinks. With the three humans and two artificial people in the narrow space, it was impossible to take a full step in any direction.

"I thought Thomas and Chance were back on the parade grounds meeting with the reporters we're going to put through the crash course," Joe yelled in Paul's ear.

"Chance said that the ones who came by told her that they would all be here for lunch, so she talked Thomas into coming and working the crowd rather than sitting around and waiting. Ian couldn't keep up with the orders, and they both have a lot of experience in bars, so they offered to help out."

67

"The bunch I'm going to be training must be included in this group. They sure aren't shy about drinking at lunch. I think I recognize that woman."

"She probably went through the camp for EarthCent Intelligence and then jumped ship for the Galactic Free Press," Paul responded.

Ian straightened up from the crouch he had assumed to get the keg connected and began filling pitchers with foam. "Just push that one under the counter there," he told Paul. "It'll settle out fine."

"Hey, guys," Chastity shouted over the bar. "Thanks for bringing reinforcements. I didn't know my whole staff drank like this."

"It's the old movies you give them for training," Joe shouted back. "Kelly has borrowed them all from those new reporters you keep sending to her office because she thought that watching them might help her prepare for press interviews. My favorite was 'It Happened One Night,' but Kelly went for 'His Girl Friday.' We both wondered why you didn't have anything more recent."

"I liked 'Nothing Sacred,' and I couldn't get any later movies because they're still in copyright," Chastity yelled through cupped hands. "It didn't matter to them that I was willing to buy a few hundred copies. They don't work that way on Earth."

"Has the paper made it to break-even yet, or is InstaSitter still covering the bills?" Paul shouted. Coincidentally, there was a sudden lull in the conversation when he began the question, and the last few words fell on dead silence.

"We would have been in the black this month if it hadn't been for those last two ransoms," Chastity replied in her normal tone of voice. The staff must have taken her

68

answer to mean that she could afford to pay for more drinks, because they all began queuing up at the bar to shake her hand and order a refill.

Joe tapped Paul on the shoulder and spoke into his ear. "We're just in the way back here. How about helping me get the empties home?"

Paul nodded, waved to Chastity, and followed Joe out the kitchen door.

A woman wedged her way up to the bar next to Chastity and asked, "Wasn't that Joe McAllister from Mac's Bones?"

"Yes," Chastity replied. "I stole you from EarthCent Intelligence, right?"

"I still feel bad about that," the woman replied, gazing sadly at her empty glass. "But it's a tough racket, right? They should have known better than to share their break room with the newspaper. It's practically the same business, after all, but we get to go to more interesting places and meet important people as reporters."

"We don't have a policy against double-dipping," Chastity said in the woman's ear, which with all the conversations going on, passed as a whisper. "If you come across anything you think they can use, go ahead and let them know. I'm pretty sure that some of the reporters I recruited from down the corridor are actually undercover agents in any case."

"You mean EarthCent Intelligence is planting agents in the paper?"

"It makes sense if you think about it. There's no better cover for spies than working as reporters, and this way, I get stuck paying all of the expenses," Chastity replied.

# Seven

"Come in, come in," Bork said, rising to meet Kelly halfway between his desk and the door to his office. The walls were decorated with an impressive collection of axes and crossbows, and a complete set of the metal-studded leather armor favored by the old Drazen berserkers was arrayed on a life-sized dummy.

"Thank you for squeezing me in on such short notice," Kelly replied, exchanging a ceremonial hug with the ambassador. "I'm a bit embarrassed to be asking this, but our EarthCent president is visiting the station, though he's taking a vacation at the moment. He complains that he doesn't get to talk to any alien diplomats on Earth since none of you bothered opening an embassy and he's hoping you can make the time to meet with him after his official reception."

"Of course," Bork said. He guided Kelly to the couch in front of his desk and then settled back into his own chair. "We were all a bit puzzled that there was no official reception when your president arrived, but then he took the honeymoon suite at the Camelot hotel and casino, so we assumed he was on vacation."

"Your intelligence people told you?"

"I saw it in the Grenouthian feed, they're very good about tracking diplomats. There was also something in my translated edition of the Galactic Free Press, though it wasn't as detailed."

"What did they leave out?" Kelly asked.

"The last Grenouthian update included video of your president eating with a woman who was identified as his mistress. It also said that she was in charge of public relations for EarthCent, and that they were here to solicit the advanced species to establish factories and educational institutions on Earth. I believe there was something about the whereabouts of the president's wandering wife as well. Did it say she was traveling with a Vergallian?"

"I don't understand how they could have found all that out," Kelly said in frustration. "I know we only discussed the visit over a secure channel or in the embassy, which we sweep for bugs all the time now, and I'm sure that the president's office takes similar precautions."

"It appears that your guests were indiscreet during their breakfast conversation this morning," Bork said. "In fact, I believe our intelligence service has contacted your intelligence service to make sure they know, though I'm sure Blythe and Clive must follow the Grenouthian feed as well.

"Oh. I had a ping from Clive a few minutes ago, but I wanted to come and see you first."

"I did a quick record search after seeing the Grenouthian report and I couldn't come up with any instances of Drazen universities operating an extension campus on an alien world. I'm afraid that our academic institutions are famously hidebound. You wouldn't believe the grief my daughter went through back home trying to get recognition for the Open University coursework she did here."

"The Drazen schools don't recognize Stryx competency exams?" Kelly asked in disbelief.

"It's a bit of a sore point for those of us in the diplomatic corps," Bork admitted. "It's not just us, though. I think the sole species whose academia fully recognizes the Stryx system is the Verlocks. There's just something in the academic mindset that makes administrators look for difficulties where none exist. Fortunately, the only people who care about academic credentials are the academics themselves, and it wouldn't have affected Minka at all if she hadn't been interested in taking an advanced degree in choral arrangement. It's just not something they offer at the Open University."

"If your universities behave like that to their own expatriates, I can't imagine they'll be interested in working with humans. The president will be very disappointed."

"There's no reason for you to deal with the official universities," Bork reassured her. "The vast majority of Drazen professionals take advanced training through their employers or the military, and it's the same with the other species, I believe. What you need to do is sit down with your president and find out specifically what skills he wants to see humans develop. Then we'll contact some Drazen consortiums which work in those fields, and ask them to bid on educating humans as if they were employees. I'm sure it will just be a matter of price and availability."

"Did you graduate from a university, Bork?"

"Certainly not. Our diplomatic service offers extensive vocational training for candidates. I'm sure I told you about the many decades I spent working in junior positions before graduating to this assignment."

"I just assumed you went to school before that."

"I completed the same basic curriculum as all Drazen children while I lived with my parents, but school is school and work is work. The diplomatic service would send me for special courses with other candidates from time to time, but those were also taught by career diplomats."

"Well, that's great news, then, and I look forward to telling the president. But there was something else I wanted to ask you about."

"Apparently your president didn't discuss it at breakfast because I thought that was everything," Bork teased her, a twinkle in his eye.

"An EarthCent president has never visited Union Station before so we wanted to make an impression with the reception. We have permission from the Stryx to hold it in the new Libbyland attraction before it's opened to the public, and since it's an Earth-themed medieval castle, I think most of the ambassadors will enjoy it. But they're only just starting to hire staff now, and the concept calls for a large number of professional reenactors."

"I'll do it," Bork said.

"What? You don't even know what it is yet."

"If it involves weapons and acting, you've come to the right place. Do you think it's easy to find reenactment gigs? My practice group has been so desperate lately that we've started playing children's parties."

"I thought you might be able to suggest where we could find actors with weapons skills who could play humans," Kelly said in embarrassment. "I've watched your demo reel many times and I'm sure if you hadn't gone into diplomacy you could have made a living as a principal, but there is the, uh, extra appendage."

"This?" Bork said incredulously, waving his tentacle behind his head. "I'll just tape it down my back like I always do when I'm playing other humanoid species. I've been a Horten spearman in more low budget dramas than I can count and the tentacle was the least of my problems. Can you guess how long I spent in a makeup chair for less than two minutes of background work?"

"I, uh, no."

"Six hours! By the time we got to the last two skin color changes they didn't even bother cleaning off the previous coat, they just sprayed a new layer on top. It was like acting in a death mask."

"I see," Kelly said, wondering how the president would feel about Drazen actors playing human reenactors for his reception.

"Speaking of Hortens, they have a large theatre group on the station that's mainly historical reenactors as well," Bork said. "We try to put aside politics when it comes to the arts, and they hire our whole group every year for their Warriors Day celebration. We usually do a skirmish from the Battle of Scort Woods or the Taking of Death's Head Castle. I've been meaning to ask Dring if he's interested in a fly-on role as a fire-breathing dragon."

"But I thought that the Drazens and the Hortens practically go to war every year over ratings for your historical broadcast series."

"Network stuff is big business. We're talking about live performances here, a completely different animal. Do you think it's easy for performance artists to find audiences? I'm sure that anything involving Libbyland will pay scale, but the truth is, most of the actors in my group would do it for a chance to dress up and storm a castle, with maybe a round of Divverflips at the end of the day."

"I guess that will work, Bork. Thank you. But I'm also counting on you to be there to meet the president and help set the tone for the other ambassadors. How can you be part of the entertainment and a guest at the same time?"

Bork looked stricken for a moment and his tentacle drooped. "How about I get one of my staff to pretend to be me? Your president would never know the difference."

"But I'll know the difference, Bork, and so will the other ambassadors."

"What sort of entertainment did you have planned? Will there be a show and then a dinner, or will it be fighting after dinner, or do you want martial activity going on in the background throughout the reception?"

"I really don't know," the ambassador admitted. "Donna does most of our planning, but since it's a new venue, I don't have anything to go by. We did visit the castle and the interior rooms aren't finished yet, so I guess the fighting will go first and then we'll hold a reception on the ramparts."

"I'm sure I can make this work," Bork said. "You tell whoever is in charge of hiring that I can deliver two medieval armies with paid-up Thark accidental dismemberment insurance, and we'll want to get in there before the reception to practice. We have five days, right?"

Kelly nodded. She couldn't remember the last time the Drazen ambassador looked so energized, so she decided to swallow her misgivings and accept the generous offer. A shrill trumpet sounded, and Bork growled in the direction of his display desk, "What is it?"

"Ambassador Czeros here to see you," the disembodied voice of the Drazen embassy secretary responded.

"Send him in," Bork said, rising to his feet.

Kelly also rose, expecting to follow the Drazen ambassador to the door to meet their colleague, but instead Bork walked over to the wall and grabbed the hilt of what looked like a very nasty broadsword. For a moment, Kelly was sure that he intended to cut down the Frunge ambassador for interrupting a conversation about acting, but it turned out that the hilt served as the handle for the door of a hidden liquor cabinet. Bork rummaged through the contents for a moment, and then came up with a bottle of red wine that looked suspiciously familiar.

"Is that the wine from the gift basket my embassy sent for your hundredth anniversary with the diplomatic service?" Kelly asked suspiciously.

"My family ate all of the fruit and the individually wrapped pieces of cheese and meat," Bork said. "We're just not big wine drinkers. In fact, I'm not sure I have the right technology to remove the stopper."

"Cork," Czeros announced, entering the office. "It's alright, I carry one with me." The ambassador reached into his belt pouch and drew out a Frunge army knife that put Joe's antique Swiss army knife to shame. Czeros pulled out a number of attachments, cursed, and then something clicked into place, leaving him holding a two-handled bottle opener with a geared worm drive and a tri-spiraled corkscrew.

"Help yourself," Bork said, handing over the bottle.

The Frunge ran a professional eye over the challenge, then he spun his complicated opener into place, held the bottle clamped between his elbow and his body, and managed to work the two levers, smoothly removing the cork.

"What happened to your old corkscrew?" Kelly asked.

Czeros handed her the open bottle, then struggled to collapse the complicated assembly and fold the individual attachments back into the handle. "This is a new product from the Frunge blade-makers," the ambassador replied.

"They combined a traditional army knife with Human bottle opening technology. It's a bit over-engineered, but it was a gift, so I'm stuck using it until it breaks."

"And what brings you here, my friend?" Bork asked politely, extending a wine goblet at the same time.

"Trouble," the Frunge grunted, giving up on getting the knife fully closed and dropping it in his belt pouch with several pointy looking bits still sticking out of the handle. He accepted the wine back from Kelly and filled the glass to the rim, emptying a good third of the bottle. "Neither of you are joining me?"

"Too early for me," Kelly replied, waving off the offer.

"Too sweet for me," Bork said, retaking his seat.

Kelly settled back down on the couch and Czeros plopped down beside her, the large goblet in one hand and the bottle in the other. He took a long swallow, which turned into a chug, and drained the glass. "You aren't likely to see me do this again for a while," he said sadly, refilling the goblet.

"Is something wrong?" Kelly asked. "Have you developed a medical problem from drinking Earth wines? I thought they were chemically very close to the wines the Frunge make from those little red berries."

"There's nothing wrong with me physically," Czeros said. "It seems that somebody informed the Frunge diplomatic service that I have a drinking problem."

"Who would do that?" Bork demanded.

"My wife," the Frunge ambassador admitted glumly. "She's also taken the shrubs to stay with her sister, and I'm stuck home with both of our ancestors creaking up a storm."

"I never got to know her that well..." Kelly began, but Czeros cut her off before she could complete her sentence.

"Of course you didn't. She's xenophobic from the tips of her hair vines down to the roots of her feet. I'm aware that I sometimes overdo it at diplomatic events, but that's because I know when I get home, I'll have to listen to her bad-mouthing all of the species I think of as friends. Imagine if you had to sleep with somebody who kept talking about how the galaxy would be a better place if all of the Humans and Drazens would just disappear."

"My understanding has always been that alien affective disorder runs much higher among the Frunge than any of the other tunnel species," Bork said. "I seem to recall from an intelligence briefing that as many as one in twenty Frunge have serious difficultly accepting the existence of aliens. It's supposedly very common in those of your people with self-fertilization in their family histories."

"We don't talk about that in public," Czeros muttered. He took another gulp of wine. "We don't talk about the inspector general either, but he or she has the power to remove me from my post. This wasn't my first choice for a career, you know, but I've tried to make the best of it and I don't want it to end with dismissal."

"When is the inspector general arriving?" Bork asked. "Are you expecting a direct confrontation or an undercover investigation?"

"Both," the Frunge ambassador replied. "Our internal investigations typically begin as undercover, and when sufficient evidence has been gathered, it's presented to the subject in an effort to avoid the need for a public hearing. I only know that it's happening because a friend who was appointed to my confidential honor court tipped me off."

"So the investigation is already under way?"

"My friend contacted me immediately after he was em-panelled and sworn to secrecy so I doubt the inspector general is here yet. But these things tend to move very quickly, in part because the internal investigations division knows how hard it is for diplomats to keep a secret," Czeros concluded, showing a flash of an ironic grin.

"What can we do to help?" Kelly asked. She eyed the bottle for a moment, as if she was considering taking it from him, but it didn't seem right to interrupt what could be his last hurrah.

"I imagine the inspector general will contact you both, probably with some idiotic cover story. They're fond of posing as official historians gathering information for either a petrification plaque or a biographical entry in the Frunge Encyclopedia of Diplomacy."

"It would help a great deal if we knew who it was ahead of time," Bork mused. "I'll ask my intelligence staff to look into it and perhaps you can request the same of your own cultural attaché."

"I can't let on that I know," Czeros said. "There could be an information leak in the opposite direction, and then my old hedge friend would be in an awkward place."

"I'll check with Clive," Kelly offered. "Maybe Libby would know something as well. Libby? Do you know if the Frunge inspector general has arrived?"

"There are no recent records of Frunge officials visiting the station," the Stryx librarian replied. "If you are asking because an inspector general has been assigned to investigate Czeros, I'm afraid I would have to deny further requests on the topic as being protected competitive information."

"Any encyclopedia salesmen?" Czeros asked, which surprised Kelly, since the alien diplomats rarely spoke directly to the Stryx in her presence.

"No, but a researcher for the Frunge Encyclopedia of Diplomacy is on the passenger manifest of the liner Deeply Rooted, which just cleared tunnel traffic control."

"Does this researcher have a name?"

"Fandaz," Libby replied helpfully. "I could pop up a hologram on Ambassador Bork's desk if he'll permit it."

"Please do," Bork said, lifting a bushy eyebrow at Kelly.

A hologram of a severe-looking Frunge woman with close-cropped hair vines wearing a black leather uniform appeared. An embroidered patch on her shoulder reminded Kelly of the emblem on the binding of her collected works of Sherlock Holmes. "Is that an inspector patch?" she asked.

"That does look rather like a Frunge inspector general's uniform, doesn't it," Libby commented innocently. "My mistake."

The hologram winked out.

"When you meet her, say something nice about the way she looks," Kelly suggested. "I've never seen a Frunge woman with such short hair and I can't imagine she gets many compliments."

"I feel better already," Czeros declared, standing up and placing his empty goblet on Bork's desk. He looked at the bottle which still contained a good third of its contents and added, "I suppose I'll just take this along with me unless you have one of those re-corking tools. No? I didn't think so."

"Well, that was interesting," Kelly remarked after the Frunge ambassador departed. "We'll have to be careful around the inspector person."

"Don't make Czeros out to be an angel," Bork warned her. "Those internal affairs types can sniff out a lie. I think the best approach would be to convince her that our friend's drinking is an act he uses to gain an advantage over the other ambassadors. We'll have to try to think up some diplomatic coups we can claim he achieved."

"I'm sure I'll come up with something," Kelly said. "So, you're guarantying two medieval-style forces of reenactors who can stage a castle siege without accidentally cutting off anybody's head and you want practice time before the reception. Is there anything else?"

"It's traditional to bring in catering for the performers," Bork hinted. "You know we Drazens will eat anything, but the Hortens have always been a bit finicky, so you may want to order from one of their restaurants."

"Horten catering. Will do." Kelly rose from the couch. "Thank you so much for your help with this. I hope your family will be attending the reception."

"Of course," Bork said, escorting the EarthCent ambassador to the door. "Before I forget, will the reception guests be in a shielded area of the castle?"

"I'm not sure," Kelly replied. "Why do you ask?"

"If there's no shielded area we won't use projectiles," the Drazen ambassador replied. "Things can go wrong in the heat of battle, er, reenactment, that is. Some of the guys specialize in arrow clouds, but we can stick with swords, stabbing spears and axes. You can never go wrong with a good axe fight."

# Eight

"I had Chance take my samples around to the upscale Horten shops and they ordered more than I can possibly make while going to school," Dorothy explained to her business mentor. "Libby even said I can sew them at the lost-and-found in my free time since it's sort of like doing schoolwork, but I'm not going to be able to keep up."

"The shopkeepers really didn't recognize that you were bringing them Horten designs that went out of fashion over three thousand years ago?" Blythe asked.

"Chance said that they didn't, and I doubt it would make a difference if they did. I'm afraid I underpriced the first batch, though. And I should have given her an order limit to stop at, but it never occurred to me that the hats would be so popular."

"Where is Chance?" Blythe asked. She looked around and shook her head at the haphazard heaps of Horten millinery material filling one of the spare rooms in the ice harvester that the McAllisters called home.

"She won't sew hats," Dorothy replied. "She made some nonsensical excuse about pricking her finger with a needle and damaging her free will, so it was clear that nothing I could say would change her mind. Chance is more of a wearer than a maker. Samuel can help me some on the weekends, not that he's very productive. But he brought Banger last time, and that little Stryx is a born hatmaker."

"Did you talk to Shaina or Brinda? I'm sure they have contacts in the Shuk who could hook you up with professionals."

"That's exactly what I'm afraid of," Dorothy admitted. "I always looked up to you and Chastity, but now that I have an opportunity to follow in your footsteps, I realize that I'm not ready to drop everything and become a business tycoon. I want to finish the program at the Open University and then maybe get a job designing clothes for a famous brand. I'm just not ready to start making contracts or telling employees what to do. I wish Metoo was here. He'd help me finish these orders and then I'd have time to think."

"I'll tell you what," Blythe said. "I'll ask Tinka to scare you up some InstaSitters who like to sew and she'll handle the payroll for you, but it's just for this one batch."

"Thank you," Dorothy said in relief. She had been hoping Blythe would propose the InstaSitter solution, but she hated to ask. "Do you have any interest in starting a fashion business? I can be your designer."

"That's more of Chastity's thing, especially shoes, but she's too busy with the newspaper these days."

"Shoes are complicated, and if you get the heel wrong somebody can break an ankle. With hats, the worst thing that can happen is it messes up your hair."

"I know some Frunge girls who would consider that worse than a broken ankle," Blythe said.

"My friend Flazint is one of them. You know, even growing up as the ambassador's daughter and watching Samuel when he was on 'Let's Make Friends,' I still feel like I know so little about the other species, and they know even less about us. It's a shame the aliens won't send their children to Libby's school. I think Mist is the only non-human or non-Stryx who ever attended."

"Are you forgetting that most of the humans on the station have their children attend education circles rather than sending them to the Stryx school? It's only the parents that are completely comfortable with AI who are willing to let their five-year-olds play with indestructible robots. I'm on Libby's alumni board, you know, and I've tried doing outreach to the other species on the station, but they always say that children are too precious to risk in experiments."

"Then why are there so many aliens in the Open University? Lots of them aren't even from the station, they come from all over."

"We get plenty of Open University students working for InstaSitter to earn pocket money, and most of them are older than you'd think," Blythe replied. "Keep in mind that Vergallian women aren't considered grown-ups until they're old enough to have children, and that doesn't happen until they're in their fifties or sixties, at least in human years. The Drazens, Frunge and Hortens may mature a little quicker than that, but the Verlocks and the Grenouthians are considered children into their hundreds. It just depends on the life-spans for the species."

"Then maybe it's good we didn't go to school with alien children since we all grow up at different rates," Dorothy concluded. "I just wish I could design clothes for them and not have to deal with the business side, especially marketing and manufacturing."

"Why don't you ask Shaina and Brinda? Since Shaina had the baby, SBJ is down to just a couple of auctions a year, and last time I saw Brinda, she seemed to be glowing a bit as well, if you know what I mean. They grew up dealing with marketing and importers and they have contacts throughout the tunnel network."

"Do you think they would?" Dorothy weighed the idea of going into business with the Hadad sisters, whom she'd known all of her life. "Do you think I should ask Jeeves too? I wouldn't want him to blame me for breaking up SBJ if they stop doing auctions altogether."

"If you want credit for the idea, the trick will be to ask Jeeves before he invites himself," Blythe predicted. "Now where is everybody? I actually came over because your mother wanted me to meet with the EarthCent public relations woman, but you're the only one home."

"Paul took them all to check out the medieval castle he's been building for Libbyland and to discuss the final arrangements for the EarthCent president's reception. I was too busy with my hat orders to go along, but I visited a few times while they were building it. Have you seen the castle yet?"

"I'm waiting for the reception myself."

"Don't get tricked into thinking that it's real stone. They used a Dollnick contractor for the castle, so it's Dolly foam construction with a stone façade." Dorothy put the final stitch in the brim of the hat, and offered it to Blythe. "What do you think?"

"I like the feel of the material. What is it made from?"

"I can't pronounce the name. I just borrowed one of the old hats it's styled after from the lost-and-found and took it to a Horten supplier. All I can say is that it comes in three grades and I took the middle one." She accepted the hat back and added it to the small stack of finished merchandise.

Beowulf barked once from the living room.

"That's his David bark," Dorothy said, her eyes lighting up. "I told David I couldn't go out tonight because I had to make hats. I'll bet he's coming to offer his help even though he worked all day."

"Anybody home?" the young man's voice called from the living room.

"We're in here," Dorothy shouted back.

"I've got food."

"Alright. We'll come out." Dorothy turned to Blythe and added, "No food allowed in the production area."

David was busily unloading the contents of a Pub Haggis catering floater under the watchful eyes of Beowulf when Dorothy and Blythe entered. "I hope you're hungry," he said, without looking up. "None of this stuff comes out right in small batches so I had to make a lot."

"What is it, exactly?" Blythe asked.

"Hi, Mrs. Oxford. It's my job interview, sort of. I'm trying out for a cook position at the new Libbyland attraction. Paul pinged me and said that everybody is on their way back here, so I changed course midway."

"These look a little like the flatbread Aisha makes," Dorothy commented, picking up a plate-sized loaf from the pile. "Wow, it's heavy, though, and it feels pretty hard. Is this a bad one?"

"It's a trencher," David explained. "It's bread, but you use it as a plate, and after the meal, you can either eat it or you can put it out for the poor or the pigs. They used to bake it in the ashes of a wood fire but I used the oven. Almost all of the medieval cooking was done over an open fire or in the embers, but the closest I could come was cooking with gas. Maybe they'll get wood in for the castle."

"Not a chance," Dorothy told him. She began setting out the trenchers around the table like regular plates. "The Stryx don't allow wood burning on the stations, and if they did, the Frunge would leave the tunnel network in protest."

"What else did people eat back then?" Blythe asked.

"I got Libby to find me some recipes from Earth history books in her library, and she said that almost everything was some sort of stew or porridge, since they conserve all the liquids that way," David replied. "It's really not all that different from the regular menu at Pub Haggis. I also made some pies with meat and vegetables since a castle kitchen would have ovens and livestock. I don't think people visiting Libbyland on vacation want to experience what it was like to be a starving peasant."

Beowulf trotted over to the door of the ice harvester, listened for a moment, and then headed down the ramp.

"They must be back," Dorothy said. She moved quickly around the table, adding silverware to either side of the bread trenchers. "Is there anything else I can do?"

"Not unless you have an ox hidden somewhere that I can roast."

"Does this mean you've decided you want the job?"

"I guess I need to find out if they want me first," David replied.

Samuel was the first one in the door, followed by Kelly and Hildy. The eleven-year-old boy immediately spotted David and assumed that some of his favorites from Pub Haggis were on the menu. The president was still talking with Paul and Joe as the three men entered.

"What I'm really looking for is time to pitch the less sympathetic air-breathers," the president reiterated. "The Drazens, Verlocks and Frunge will talk to me with or without the reception. It's the Hortens, the Grenouthians and the Dollnicks I'm worried about."

"We could drop the portico and block the other exits," Paul suggested. "Castles are at least as good at keeping people in as they are at keeping them out."

"That's an interesting idea," the president mused.

"Enough," Hildy said, eyeing the men with disgust. "Haven't you ever heard that the way to an alien's heart is through his stomach?"

"You think we'll win them over with medieval food?" the president asked in surprise.

"While you men were having a good time arguing the merits of primitive weapons systems, Kelly has been filling me in on alien delicacies," Hildy replied. "Every species, no matter how wealthy, ends up with some specialty food items they can't get enough of, even if they have to create the shortage themselves. Didn't you tell me that when you were ambassador, the Grenouthians on your station threw a party that cost more than EarthCent's budget, all to celebrate some perfect piece of fruit?"

"That's right," the president acknowledged. "They wanted to show it off to everybody, and then in order to give a piece to each of the guests it wouldn't poison, they sliced it so thinly that the individual servings were barely a damp spot on the plate. Yet they all carried on about how it was the best thing they'd ever tasted."

"The promise of a battle reenactment will get them to show up, but it's the food that will make them take you seriously," Kelly said. "Just make sure they understand that there's more to come, or they'll be gone before you can get a commitment for an individual meeting. We have friends in the merchant community who can get a hold of whatever you need in a hurry if you have a budget for it."

"Don't you have some rich friends who could help out?" the president suggested.

"That would be me," Blythe said, stepping forward. "The ambassador invited me to stop by and meet with Ms. Greuen. I don't have a problem with financing some culinary bribes for alien diplomats as long as you have specific goals. If it's just to make a good impression, don't bother."

"Sit here next to me and we can discuss it while eating," the president suggested, pulling out a chair for Blythe. "By the way, you look much younger than your hologram." Hildy winked and gave the president a thumbs-up before taking a seat across the table. Everybody else pulled out chairs, and David began to circulate the serving plates.

"In case you didn't know, the flat bread things are trenchers and you eat off of them," Dorothy announced. "After the meal you can eat the bread or give them to Beowulf."

"Trencherman," Kelly said. "A hearty eater. It was seven down in last week's crossword."

"When am I going to meet this Walter fellow who creates the puzzles?" the president asked. "I'd like to wring his—hand."

"I don't know what it is with diplomats and crossword puzzles," Hildy said, poking at her trencher with a fork. "It seems that all of you are obsessed with them."

"I've been thinking about that myself, especially since Kelly started waking me up in the middle of the night with clues she can't figure out," Joe replied. "Diplomats all have to learn to say the same thing over and over again in different ways so they can keep asking for what they want without sounding like a recorded loop. For them, word games are like practice."

"I only wake you up because I love you," Kelly protested.

"You love Libby too, Mom," Samuel said. "Why not ask her?"

"That would be cheating," his mother explained.

"Why is asking Libby cheating and asking Dad not cheating?" her son persisted. "I ask Banger questions all the time, though he's pretty busy with his own Stryx stuff now."

"It's because Libby is so much smar—she has a perfect memory," Kelly amended herself hastily. "Did you try this meat pie, Joe?"

"Banger has a perfect memory too," Samuel said. "I had to teach him how to forget things."

"You what?" the president asked. He looked up so suddenly that some of the stew he was ladling onto his trencher ended up on the table.

"It's my job," the boy said proudly. "I taught Banger how to be human."

"Ah, you must attend the experimental school run by the station librarian that I've heard so much about," the president said, with a significant look at the ambassador. "I knew that the children could pay their way by working with the young Stryx, but I didn't know that teaching them to be human was the goal."

"Is that how Libby explained it when you started at her school?" Kelly asked. "That's not what Dorothy told me."

"I don't remember," the boy replied. "I think she said something about Banger needing a friend to help him fit in at school. What's the weird food?"

"Barley porridge with onions and carrots," David said. "It's the sort of thing the working people ate every day, especially if they couldn't get bread."

"It needs salt," Samuel said, after tasting a mouthful.

"Salt was too expensive for poor people to use with every meal in lots of places," David told him. "Their diets varied according to the season and region they lived in as well. In colder areas, they ate a lot of beets, oats and turnips, plus whatever they could manage from livestock, like milk, cheese and eggs. But they only got to eat fresh fruit and garden vegetables in season because their preservation methods were based on drying or pickling."

"How about beans?" Hildy asked. "My mother always had beans soaking in the kitchen."

"Beans and peas were common food for poor people," David said. "Anything that could be dried and preserved was an important part of the diet, even fish in coastal areas. I never really thought about visiting Earth before I started learning about the food, but now I'm curious to see all the different agricultural regions. It's not like the ag decks on the station where the farmers just set the climate controls to whatever they need."

"No, it's not," the president confirmed. "Weather is one of the main topics of conversation on Earth, if you can believe that. What was in that tasty stew?"

"Salt cod," David said. "I would have made more, but apparently the Verlocks buy up most of the imports that reach the station. Ian special-orders a crate once in a while for the restaurant, mainly to make pies. And my pies aren't really authentic, or maybe you could say they're late medieval, because the crust is edible. Early pie crusts were just a thick flour and water casing to allow the food to be cooked in a stone oven without drying out. The crust also preserved the food by providing an air-tight wrapper until it was broken open, but it was too hard for all but the poorest people to try eating it."

"The aliens will never know the difference as long as it looks right," Paul commented. "You know, I've been working with Jeeves on the Libbyland attractions ever since we did the Physics Ride together, but the concept for the medieval castle is completely different, more like a living museum. It's good you did all the research on how food was cooked because that's more important than how it comes out. We want visitors to see what life in a castle was like around a thousand years ago."

"You mean you're really looking for reenactors rather than cooks?"

"Well, yes. But we also need a cook to teach them how to act. They'll have to learn to make food, but depending on who is visiting the castle that day, it might not get eaten."

Beowulf barked to remind everybody of his availability.

"So you're copying the model of tourist attractions on Earth," Hildy said. "I grew up near a port where they had an old wooden warship, with actors dressed in period costumes who would explain the cannons and rigging."

"What's rigging?" Samuel asked.

"All of the parts that the ship used to catch the wind for sailing. You know what masts and sails are, right?"

The boy nodded.

"The ropes, or cordage, were just as important. Some of the ropes were permanent, they basically held the masts in place so they didn't fall over or snap off in the wind. Other ropes were attached to all the other wood parts, I think they were called spars or booms, and they were used to control the sails."

"Spars include all of the wood poles," Joe interjected. "Masts are the vertical spars, booms are the horizontal ones, though there were a lot of special names for each specific position in the rigging. When a new sailor came onboard a ship, the first thing they would do is teach him which ropes did what."

"I see that expression in books all the time, 'teaching somebody the ropes,' but I never knew where it came from," Kelly said. "I bet it shows up in a crossword puzzle one of these days."

# Nine

"Thank you for the invitation to your presidential reception, Mrs. Ambassador. You've made my job so much easier."

"When I heard that a Frunge encyclopedia researcher was on the station to honor our colleague, I wanted to do something to help," Kelly replied. "You might think it petty of me to keep score, but I hope to begin paying down my debt to Ambassador Czeros for all the good turns he's done for humanity, not to mention the diplomatic community at large."

"Is that so?" the undercover Frunge inspector general said, sounding entirely unimpressed. "So you have nothing but good to say about him?"

"Oh, that wouldn't be realistic. Perhaps we could find a place a little more private to talk?" Kelly put on her best diplomatic smile as she drew Fandaz away from the crenellated battlement where the guests were gathering to watch the promised action. "Was there something special you wanted to ask?"

"Our encyclopedia endeavors to offer a balanced portrait of the outstanding Frunge diplomats we choose to include," Fandaz said. "I'm quite aware of the contributions Czeros has made to the forest from the official records, but it's the shape of the individual tree that I'm hoping to capture. How he gets along with his fellow diplomats, how he forwards the Frunge cause through unofficial channels, how he differs from the stereotypical wooden ambassadors our people tend to produce."

"I'm sure you know that he considered becoming a singer before dedicating himself to public service," Kelly said. "We all count on him for entertainment at parties." She crossed her fingers behind her back, hoping the inspector would conflate her two statements and assume that Czeros entertained his colleagues by singing.

"I didn't know that about him," Fandaz said, scratching at the root of a stubby hair vine. "I have heard some colorful stories about his cross-species feats of alcohol consumption."

"Oh, you know about that already." Kelly exhaled deeply as if she'd been deflated and tried to look guilty. In reality, she was summoning up all of her latent acting skills for the performance she had cooked up after consultation with Blythe and Clive. "Would it be possible to leave that incident out of your encyclopedia, or at least not to mention my name and the station? I understand why you'd see it as such an important insight into his character, but it's more than a little embarrassing to me, and it could impact my career if word gets out."

"I'm not sure if we're talking about the same thing here," the inspector general said, her eyes taking on a crafty shine. "Just describe the events to me the way you remember them."

"Well, I'm sure you know about it already, but back when my people decided we should start an intelligence service, I made the mistake of inviting Czeros to a party at my home. As you alluded to, he's well known for his ability to imbibe quantities of alcohol while remaining perfectly sober."

"He is?"

"On that night, he kept us all so amused that I guess we let our guards down and tried to match him drink-for-drink, forgetting that he was one of you rather than one of us. I don't have to tell you how charming he can be. The next morning when I awoke, I realized that we had revealed all of our intelligence secrets to Czeros, including the identities of our agency director and steering committee members. He never embarrassed us by mentioning it again, but I'm sure it all ended up in your official records. I suspect that's why we were unable to go into an intelligence partnership with the Frunge and had to settle for the Drazens."

"That's not—there was something—I'll have to check the archives again," Fandaz sputtered. "He remains sober, you say?"

"Oh, yes," Kelly declared ruefully. "He won't trick me again. At first I assumed that Frunge were simply immune to alcohol, being a different species and all, but eventually I realized that Czeros pretends to drink more than he actually does. He's such a consummate actor that I'll bet he could fool his own wife."

"This is useful information, but I'll need to confirm it with his other colleagues, of course."

"Of course," Kelly agreed, leading the inspector general back towards the mob of guests. The alien dignitaries were hanging over the wall and adding their own insults to those thrown back and forth between the two parties of would-be warriors. "But in fairness, I think you should take anything the Drazen or Verlock ambassadors have to say with a grain of salt. Czeros always gets the best of them in meetings."

"Drazen and Verlock," Fandaz said, making a mental note to interview them. "That's Srythlan and Bork?"

"Yes, but you have them backwards. Bork is the Drazen."

"Is that him over there?"

"No, that's Herl. I think he's involved in the entertainment business," Kelly fibbed. "Bork will be joining the party just as soon as he gets killed."

"What?" Fandaz stared at the ambassador in horror.

"On the battlefield," Kelly explained, and on receiving a blank look, she continued to elucidate. "We wanted to use the castle for our president's reception but they haven't begun hiring reenactors yet. So we asked the Drazens and the Hortens to help show how humans attacked and defended their castles a thousand years ago."

"I see," the inspector general said. "Can I assume that they'll be using Frunge blades?"

"We can't control that, of course, but I know that the Frunge blade sellers do good business on our market deck," Kelly replied cautiously. "I plan to ask Czeros for help when it comes to acquiring weapons to decorate the castle's great hall."

Fandaz thanked the ambassador and moved off in search of Srythlan. Kelly watched her go with relief, and then headed for the group of alien ambassadors gathered around the president. Incredibly, he had them all eating out of his hand.

"Now, try this one," the president said, extending what looked like an artisanal chocolate to the new Vergallian ambassador, who leaned forward and took the candy between her brilliant white teeth. Kelly blinked to make sure she wasn't imagining things, but Aaluna was purring like a kitten on catnip.

"Let somebody else get in there," the Dollnick ambassador complained, picking up the high-caste Vergallian with his lower set of arms and moving her to the side.

"Ah, Ambassador Crute," the president said. "I believe that Ms. Greuen blew a hole in our budget shopping just for you." He turned to the public relations expert, who already had a small silver bag ready to hand him. "One of my greatest disappointments back in my days as an ambassador was my inability to participate in the wonderful meals at the Dollnick embassy due to my inferior digestive system. I spent many an evening trying to imagine the taste of Sheezle larvae, but I had to settle for devouring them with my eyes."

"Sheezle larvae?" All four of Crute's hands were trembling as he accepted the bag of bugs from the president. "When I took over the Dollnick embassy on this station, I was horrified to learn that the previous ambassador had so abused the common table that the Council of Princes removed Sheezle larvae from our budget. I haven't tasted one since I visited the homeworld. Please forgive my emotional outburst. I need to be alone for a moment."

"More, more," Ambassador Aaluna said, pointing at her mouth and pouting like a child. The president obliged her with another dainty from the box that Hildy held at the ready.

"It's starting," somebody called out, and the guests who had been milling around the president reluctantly moved to join those who were already lining the battlements.

The president allowed himself to be towed along by the Vergallian ambassador, who was torn between her appetite for the expensive sweets and her natural desire to see a bunch of men bashing at each other with primitive weapons. Kelly spotted Samuel and Blythe's children sitting on the framework of a catapult that gave them an unobstructed view, so she headed over to see if she could find the rest of the family. In the open field below the castle's walls, the performance began.

"Deliver the Holy Grail or die!" cried a giant Horten warrior, who wore a horned hat that looked like an opera prop.

"For England and the Pope!" thundered back one of the Drazen defenders, brandishing a war axe.

The two sides rushed to meet each other with a clash of metal, and the battle lines quickly dissolved into a hundred individual duels. Immersive cameras floated above the combatants, gathering footage for the news or personal audition reels, but the battle was otherwise more realistic than Kelly had imagined.

After a few minutes, the fighters on both sides broke apart as if by prior agreement, and the leaders of the two forces met at the center of the field. A protracted duel between an axe-wielding Drazen and the Horten sword master featured so many deadly blows and thrusts blocked at the last instant that Kelly was terrified that one of the actors would really die. Then the giant Horten drove his broadsword through the chest of the Papist Drazen, who threw his arms out theatrically and declared, "Let death be my bride tonight," before collapsing.

As the general fighting resumed to a round of applause from the guests, a low wooden cart drawn by two figures in cassocks emerged from the castle. The monks loaded the dead defender's corpse, and then disappeared from sight under the wall.

"I guess Bork bought the farm," Joe said cheerfully, putting his arms around Kelly from behind. "I recognize that line from his part in the Drazen immersive that got cancelled. But who gave him that battle cry about the Pope and England?"

"The English were Catholics until the 1500's," Kelly said defensively. "The medieval period was pretty much over by the time they went independent."

"And did you give the Horten the line about the Holy Grail?"

"Apparently they have to yell a slogan or they can't start fighting. It was either that or something about offending a lady's honor. I just hope that Bork didn't get hurt when he was killed in the duel."

Despite all of the noise coming from the battlefield, Joe lowered his voice to ask, "How did it go with the inspector general?"

Kelly looked around before replying. "I think she believed me. Clive pointed out that people usually take you at your word when you speak badly about yourself, and the records will support the story, since the Frunge and everybody else were eavesdropping on our first intelligence steering committee meeting."

"I watered down a couple of bottles of wine with grape juice and water, and Paul is keeping them handy below the bar so he can always be prepared to serve a glass. Czeros and the inspector general are the only Frunge in attendance, so if Paul sees her coming up behind Czeros at the bar, he'll give a diluted bottle to the ambassador and then serve her from a special blend with the same label."

"Special blend?"

"I added some grain alcohol to one bottle, just to punch it up a bit. If the inspector drinks it, she's going to come away thinking that Czeros must have an iron head."

After twenty minutes of pitched battle, the Horten Vikings withdrew under a barrage of Drazen Saxon insults. Then one of the defenders realized that the catering had arrived, and the Drazens hastened after their enemies to the staging area.

"Look at the president and Hildy," Joe said, nudging his wife. "They've got the ambassadors following them around like puppies."

"I just hope he gets them all to agree to meetings before he runs out of treats," Kelly replied. "Hi, Bork. You were fantastic."

"Did you like my old sword-between-the-arm-and-body trick?" the Drazen ambassador inquired. "I realized early on that to get featured background work on my vacations, I had to specialize. I'm well known for getting killed." He paused and glanced around. "How's our joint misinformation operation going?"

"I talked to the inspector general already so she'll be looking for you. I saw her heading off in Srythlan's direction before the fighting began. The ambassador is going to speak to her at the regular Verlock cadence rather than speeding himself up. He has a story prepared about how Czeros outsmarted him during the Carnival election and it involves a lot of numbers. I can't imagine she'll last through the whole thing."

"That was some pretty fancy axe play," Joe complimented Bork. "I thought that between his reach and the sword, that giant Horten would make short work of you."

"The Hortens traditionally fight in heavy armor so their swordsmen focus on brute force rather than finesse," the Drazen explained. "I was able to keep closing with him, and he didn't want to back off to make space for fear of looking like he was retreating."

"Where did you all get the protective gear you were wearing?" Kelly asked. "It looked like something from human history."

"Jeeves had it made up for us out of expanded polyvinyl chloride. According to the station librarian, most humans at the time would have been wearing boiled leather armor with metal plates attached, but with the dull weapons, we figured we could do without the extra weight of the plates. Jeeves is letting us keep it in case we play the castle again."

Kelly turned to Joe and asked, "Expanded polyvinyl chloride?"

"It's a plastic substitute for leather. Our combat boots were made out of it, but they called it Naugahyde."

"Mom," Dorothy interrupted. "The president is looking for you."

"Coming," Kelly said. "Bork, the inspector general is heading this way. Are you ready?"

"Act two, coming up," the Drazen reassured her.

Kelly did her best to look glum as she nodded at the Frunge woman in passing, and then she scanned the crowd for the president. At first the ambassador couldn't spot him anywhere, but then she saw a hand waving to her from a crowd of giant bunnies. As she approached, the Grenouthians moved away, all of them intent on a small box their ambassador was carrying.

"Nothing like getting the tough customers out of the way first," the president commented to Kelly. "The Vergallians, the Dollnicks and the Grenouthians have all agreed to meetings. You've already lined up the Verlocks, Drazens and Frunge, so that just leaves the Hortens, unless we're going to extend the invitation to the compatible off-network species."

102

"I don't think there's a need for that, Mr. President," Kelly replied. "And you didn't mention the Cherts, though I saw some empty spaces in the prime viewing spots at the wall so I assume they're lurking about somewhere."

"I couldn't find anything to impress the Hortens," Hildy admitted. "Their food fetishes all revolve around cleanliness and quantity rather than taste and rarity. They don't use cosmetic products, their technology is at least on the level of the Drazens, and according to our intelligence reports, they tend not to be interested in new things."

"Except for games," Kelly said, reaching in her purse. "My mother is an antiquing fanatic and she keeps sending my son these portable electronic games. They're obsolete, of course, and he only plays them for a week or two before he gets bored. This one has something to do with aliens from space invading Earth, though from what I can see, they mainly move back and forth in a line waiting to get shot." She passed the hand-held device to the president and rooted around her purse again. "This one is about building a continuous wall out of falling bricks."

"It may work," the president said. "I remember the Horten ambassador on Void Station was an avid gamer. The only time he would talk to me was in meetings about interspecies tournaments. If you can round up this Ortha fellow, I'll try to make the sale."

"I think he found out that we ordered Horten take-out for the attacking army, so he snuck out to congratulate them after the battle," Kelly said. "I doubt he'll be very cooperative if I pull him away from food, but the only active lift tube near here is in the courtyard, so if you wait down there he can't sneak past you."

"That's good," the president said. "I better practice with these doohickeys while I'm waiting so I can explain what they do. I'm not much for building walls so I'll stick with this invading aliens game."

"Space Invaders," Kelly told him. She extended the device still in her possession to Hildy, and asked, "Would you like Tetris?"

Hildy laughed and took the game.

"What's so funny?" Kelly asked.

"Just something about the way you said it reminded me of the world's most successful greeting card. You remember things like that if you've worked in marketing."

"What was it?"

"Well, there was a picture, of course, so words don't do it justice. It showed a young man and a young woman sitting beneath a tree in the country, and the young man had a book open. The caption shows that he asked the woman, 'Do you like Kipling?', and she replies, 'I don't know, you naughty boy. I've never Kipled!'"

"That's pretty funny, though the truth is that Joe is the one in our family who likes Kipling," Kelly said. The president and his mistress looked at the EarthCent ambassador strangely. "The war stories, I mean. Kipling wrote a lot of British Empire war stories."

"Ah, glad to hear you didn't mean the other Kipling," the president said, causing Kelly to blush up to her ears. "We'll be downstairs building walls and shooting aliens if you see the Horten ambassador before we do."

Kelly looked around for Srythlan to check on how his interview with the inspector general had gone. Instead she spotted the Frunge woman heading towards the bar, looking very much like she needed a drink. As planned, Czeros was already there, chatting with Paul, who wore a period costume. As the inspector general approached, the

Frunge ambassador ostentatiously lifted a full bottle of wine to his lips and guzzled the contents.

"You cut quite a figure as an ambassador," Fandaz said drily, stepping up next to Czeros. She turned to address Paul. "Could I have one of those?"

"One bottle coming up," Paul said cheerily. "You Frunge can sure hold your alcohol."

"Just a glass for me," the inspector general hastened to correct him. She surreptitiously compared the label on the empty bottle that Czeros still held with the one Paul poured for her. Then she sniffed the contents of her glass suspiciously, took a sip, and stared in amazement.

"Greetings and salutations," Czeros said to the inspector general. "What an efficient and modern-looking young lady you are. Is it possible you are one of Dorothy's school friends?"

Fandaz's closely shorn hair vines turned bright green as the chlorophyll rushed to the surface at the unexpected compliment. She gulped her fortified wine to buy time, and Paul promptly refilled the glass.

"I'm a researcher for the Petrification Bureau," the inspector general stammered. "I mean, the Frunge Encyclopedia of Diplomacy," she corrected herself.

"Ah, that makes more sense," Czeros said gallantly. "I've never met a Frunge who did less to remind me of our petrified ancestors. You seem to know who I am already, so is it possible you were planning on interviewing me about one of my illustrious colleagues? I owe so much to so many mentors that it would be a great honor for me to participate in gilding their legacies."

Fandaz took a sip from her newly filled glass and felt the alcohol going directly to her brain. She wasn't much of a drinker to start with, and the wine she had seen the ambassador pouring back was incredibly strong. "How did you get down a whole bottle of this stuff?" the inspector general gasped before she could stop herself.

"Human wine?" Czeros asked, as if surprised by the question. "I don't really care for it, but they put such a strong focus on social drinking in our diplomatic training that I developed a tolerance for the intoxicating beverages of many species. I just lost a friendly bet with our bartender, as I was sure that the Hortens would put those scrofulous Drazen defenders to flight. Did we say two bottles?"

"I think it was three, but I guess I can let you off the hook," Paul said. He retrieved another one of the diluted bottles of wine and handed it to Czeros, who with a resigned expression chugged half of the contents.

Fandaz took another sip from her glass and felt wobbly on her feet.

"So which one of my colleagues did you wish to interview me about?" Czeros continued, taking the inspector general by the elbow and guiding her to a faux-stone bench in a private alcove. "Is it Cebrat?" he asked, naming the Frunge who his friend on the honor court had identified as the chief judge. "I've always said that of all my seniors, Cebrat would be the first to be immortalized in the Encyclopedia. Did you know I was his secretary not so many years ago? No, that would be ancient history to a young sapling like you."

"Is the light in here too strong?" Fandaz slurred, polishing off her wine in an attempt to rehydrate. "I feel like I'm drying out."

"It is a bit much in the blue part of the spectrum," Czeros acknowledged. "Perhaps it would be best if I escorted you to a quiet grove on our deck where you can take your shoes off and stick your roots in the mud."

# Ten

"I hope you all had a good lunch and you're ready to do some serious work." Thomas paused for the polite replies and counted up the number of Galactic Free Press correspondents attending the hastily designed one-week course in Mac's Bones. "We're just waiting for two more people to show up before we get started."

"What are you going to do to us?" a woman in her mid-thirties asked nervously. "I've heard of kidnap training for business executives where the instructors attack you and threaten you with weapons."

"We're not going to do any of that," Thomas reassured her. "None of you are trained fighters, and as humans, you're at a disadvantage against most of the species who might want to kidnap or otherwise harm you. Our job is to convince you not to take stupid chances in pursuit of a story that at best might hold a reader's attention through half a bowl of breakfast cereal."

"So if somebody does try to kidnap me, should I just give up?" the woman persisted. "Why do those other training courses focus on attacks and escapes?"

"I'm sure they teach other things as well. The threat of physical violence in training programs is there to condition you to deal with the stress of losing control, so you won't immediately panic if it happens for real."

"Couldn't we just have lectures and a pop quiz?" a man followed up. "I thought the immersive you showed this morning about eating out on alien worlds was really educational." The other reporters laughed nervously.

"We show that immersive to all of our EarthCent Intelligence recruits as well. For humans traveling on alien worlds, eating the local food is a much greater hazard than kidnapping. I'm told that last year your paper's correspondents suffered almost three thousand cases of food poisoning, or around four incidents per reporter in the field. Joe?"

"Huddle up here, people." The owner of Mac's Bones clapped sharply and opened a large, flat case. "If you don't get anything else out of this class, at least you can brag about being the first humans equipped with food poisoning scanners. You've probably seen similar rings in Drazen markets if you've traveled in their space, but these were specially commissioned by EarthCent Intelligence and the Galactic Free Press. The first batch from the Chintoo orbital arrived just yesterday."

"I've seen Drazens use those rings," an older correspondent said. "I thought our diets were too limited to bother with scanning food for problems. It's just going to reject everything."

"How many times did you get sick gambling on a piece of alien fruit last year?" Joe asked.

"Three," the man admitted ruefully.

"So that makes three times somebody won't get sick once the rings are trained."

"What do you mean? We have to teach the scanners what we can and can't eat?"

"That's pretty much how it works," Joe replied. "The rings have been programmed to spot known toxins, and I hope you all know better than to try eating any alien meats, but some of the fruits and grains can keep you alive, especially if you boil them first. Your best bet traveling places without a human presence is to order vegan off of the Vergallian menu."

"Bob Steelforth, Galactic Free Press," a young man announced. The older reporters all laughed at his reflexive statement of credentials before asking a question. "But what did all of the human workers on alien worlds eat when they first arrived?"

"Factory food and vat-grown meats for the main part, until they could get modified human crops growing on those worlds," Joe replied. "Of course, these days the space elevators on Earth allow for agricultural exports, especially to mining colonies and terraforming projects. Otherwise, producing factory food for a different species isn't much of a challenge for any of the advanced civilizations because they've been doing it for a very long time. The issue only comes up when you're traveling places that don't typically get human visitors."

"Which is most of the places you'll go as a correspondent if they ever let you off Union Station," another reporter told Steelforth.

"Our intestinal tracks are full of bacteria that do most of the heavy lifting," Joe continued. "I'm told that in ten thousand years or so, they'll adapt to the environments we live in and we'll be able to eat like the Drazens. In the meantime, the rings will learn from your reactions, and when you're back on the station, we'll download the information and provide an update with the latest consensus on what's safe to eat."

"So we're guinea pigs," a woman commented brightly. She didn't appear to be particularly upset by the concept.

"That's right. By next year, we hope the rings will be smart enough that you'll be able to walk into an alien pub and find something safe to eat on the buffet."

"A human, a Vergallian and a Drazen walked into a bar," another of the reporters began in jest.

"And all three of them asked me to dance," Chance interrupted, arriving late as usual. "If I knew you were giving out jewelry today, I would have come early."

"They're food and poison scanners," Thomas told her. "We don't need them."

"Of course we do. If they become as popular with humans as the rings the Drazen travelers wear, we'll stick out like sore thumbs if we don't have one."

"She's got a point, and we've got plenty of these to go around," Joe said. "Just remember not to let anybody download the results or you'll both create a bunch of false negatives for the database."

The correspondents crowded around and eagerly selected rings for themselves, the free price being the main motivation. Then Chance took over, handing out the scripts she'd transcribed from holo-recordings with Chastity and Walter.

"What's this?" asked an older woman. Her name tag identified her as Penelope Ross, alien correspondent for Horten Four.

"It's your assignment for this afternoon. EarthCent Intelligence has found that role-playing is the best way to train for personal encounters, including the sort that lead to a kidnapping. Later in the week, we'll practice unscripted scenarios to see how well you've internalized the course material from the morning sessions. Today, we'll be walking you through actual kidnappings."

"I'll turn on the hologram," Thomas said. He issued a silent instruction, and an interior scene from an empty bar on an unidentified orbital popped into view in front of the surprised students. "This original video was recorded through the implant of one of the correspondents kidnapped by pirates off of a frontier orbital on the boundary between Sharf space and the tunnel network. The hologram was synthesized for us by our Stryx librarian, who also added a humanoid place-holder that shows the position of the victim who recorded the scene."

"First we'll show the action without the audio, just so you can see how the events played out," Chance said. "Then we'll have some of you take the places of the individuals in the hologram and speak their parts. Thanks to the high recording capacity of the implants provided to you by your employer, we can walk you through all four of the recent kidnappings to hit the paper."

"This is spooky," somebody muttered.

"Does everybody have a good view?" Thomas inquired. "Alright, I'm starting the action."

In a blink of the eye, the hologram of the bar scene went from deserted to packed with customers. Most of the crowd were humanoid, primarily Hortens, though there were a good number of Drazens, Gem, and a couple of dried-out looking Frunge. A humanoid figure with long black hair sitting at a table with her back to the viewers was outlined in white at the front of the hologram.

"The figure with the white highlight is Katya Wysecki, one of the reporters ransomed back from pirates this year," Joe interjected.

Katya's form extended an arm and raised a glass from the table, though they couldn't see her drink it since her back was towards them. Given the crowded bar, it seemed strange that she was alone at a table that could seat at least four, and a full minute passed with no more action than patrons and waitresses moving past the table.

"While we're waiting for the excitement to start, what is she doing right?" Thomas asked.

"She's in a public place," somebody replied.

"Very good," the artificial person confirmed. "Now what is she doing wrong? Nobody? Chance?"

"The level of her drink isn't getting any lower," Chance observed. "Anybody who watched her could tell that she was faking. If you're worried about getting drunk, either spill it out on the floor or order a drink without alcohol."

"What else?" Thomas inquired. "Come on, this is an easy one. Senior Correspondent Daggert must have mentioned it at least ten times in his lecture this morning."

"She's alone?" Bob said uncertainly.

"Exactly," Thomas replied.

Three Hortens loomed into the hologram from somewhere behind the correspondent. One of them sat down beside her, so he also appeared as an interpolated white outline, but the other two sat across from her, giving the implant plenty to record. Both were heavily tattooed, and the female of the pair had a number of gemstones studded about her face. Nobody would mistake them for anything other than pirates.

As soon as the newcomers sat, a waitress approached the table. She remained still for a moment while taking their order, swatted away the hand of the white-outlined figure sitting next to Katya, and then departed. The Horten across from the correspondent began speaking and gesturing with his hands, and after a long speech, the female next to him said something. Then both of the pirates whose faces were visible laughed long and hard.

After that, Katya must have talked at length, because the pirates across from her were looking intently in her direction and occasionally nodding, with the male interrupting just once. Finally, the waitress returned with three drinks, two a deep green color for the males, and something split into brown and white levels, which went to the female. The correspondent handed the waitress a twenty-cred coin, and the pirates nodded their appreciation. The drinks disappeared rapidly as the conversation was batted back and forth, then all four of the figures rose and exited. The hologram blinked and returned to its original state, showing an empty bar.

"So she went with them willingly!" somebody exclaimed.

"Yes," Thomas said. "In three of the four kidnappings you'll see, the correspondents placed themselves in the hands of the kidnappers while pursuing a story. The exception was a war correspondent on a Vergallian world who was caught on foot after his quadruped threw a shoe and lamed."

"Five of you should have scripts for the first hologram," Chance said. "We'll be starting just before the pirates enter, so whoever is playing Katya, please take your place, and the rest of you join her as you see your characters appear."

Penelope walked into the hologram and disappeared from view.

"Maybe we should turn down the power on the projection so they aren't hidden," Joe ventured.

"It works better like this," Chance asserted. "Chastity and Walter watched while we tried it a few different ways with InstaSitters."

"I'm Male Pirate #1," Bob said. "Does that make me the guy next to Katya or across from her?"

"Across from her," Chance answered. "Everybody ready? Your implant will beep when it's your turn to talk. Walk to your character in the hologram and just read the lines."

The action started, and with a push and a stumble, the three correspondents playing pirates entered the hologram and disappeared. "You're Katya?" Bob's voice asked, as the pirate he represented moved into the booth.

"That's right," Penelope replied. "I was told you could help me."

"One hand washes the other," Bob said gruffly.

"Let me buy the first round," Penelope offered, as the waitress approached the table.

"What will you have," asked a man's voice, in perfect lip-sync with the Horten waitress.

"Venom," Bob replied.

"Same here," another man said.

"Heaven and Hell," the woman playing the female Horten requested.

"Try that again and you'll be missing a hand," growled the man playing the waitress when the pirate next to Katya attempted a butt pat.

Everybody watching the hologram gave a brief laugh.

"Look," Bob's voice proclaimed, as the male pirate across from Katya leaned forward. "We don't have much to do with Humans out here, and we don't trust people whose skin color doesn't show anything. Do you think I covered my face with tattoos because I love my mother? All I know about you is from our mutual contact, and she said you're looking to embed with a trustworthy ship of freebooters to write a journalistic piece. Hey, I enjoy publicity as much as the next pirate, but maybe you're just a freelancer hoping for a story that will land you a job. I don't put my head on the chopping block for every Human that walks into a bar."

"With a Dollnick and a Vergallian," interjected the voice that was playing the female pirate.

"Laughs loud and long," Bob read. "Oh, sorry." All three of the correspondents playing pirates attempted to laugh, and Penelope joined in.

"The way I heard it, it was a human, a Vergallian and a Horten," Penelope read when they stopped laughing. If it had been meant as a joke, it fell flat. "I work for the Galactic Free Press. That's the biggest human news organization outside of Earth, and we must have a dozen correspondents out here just to cover the Brotherhood. I'm full-time on salary with paid expenses, so you can thank my employers for those drinks when they come. Don't confuse me with some stringer who's trying to break into the news business with immersive footage to sell to the Grenouthians. The bunnies will run anything they can get their hands on, but they'd never support a field correspondent who wasn't born with a pouch and big, floppy ears."

"Keep talking," Bob read from his script.

"I can promise you a major feature," Penelope continued in the role of the kidnapped correspondent. "No names, of course, unless you want them, but I'll tell your stories in your own words. How you got into this line of work, what challenges you face, everything that gets across the true feeling of what you do. I'm not here to judge anybody."

The waitress arrived with the drinks, and the incongruous voice playing her grunted, "Fifteen creds."

"Keep it," Penelope said, as Katya's hologram handed over a twenty-cred piece.

"Bright blood," the three pirates declared in acknowledgement of Katya paying for the drinks.

"There's more where that came from," Penelope said, lifting her own glass and actually drinking from it this time.

"I've always had a healthy interest in the news business," said the voice playing the pirate sitting by Katya's side. "How does a newbie species like the Humans come up with the money to compete with the Grenouthians?"

"Our publisher has deep pockets," Penelope read from her script. "She's a partner in the most successful human business on the stations."

"Is that so?" Bob said. The hologram of the pirate across from Katya that the young reporter was giving voice to drained his glass. "Drink up, shipmates. I've heard all I need. Welcome to our crew, Ms. Whacky."

"Wysecki," Penelope corrected him.

"Suit yourself," Bob replied magnanimously, rising from the table. The four exited the hologram together.

"Does anybody want to tell us what Ms. Wysecki got wrong?" Thomas asked.

"She may as well have begged them to kidnap her," one of the correspondents observed.

"Be specific," Thomas said.

"Well, she was the only human in a Horten pirate bar and she went in without backup. Then she pointed out something they clearly knew already, that it's not worth kidnapping stringers collecting video for the Grenouthians because the bunnies would never pay a single cred to get them released. Then she told them that the Galactic Free Press treats her like a valuable employee, and when the pirate followed up to find out if the paper was solvent, she

116

blabbed that the publisher is rich. I would have kidnapped her myself if I was in their shoes."

"We started with this reenactment because the lessons are so obvious and I'm sure you've all absorbed them," Thomas said. "Before we move on to the next hologram, which believe it or not starts with a correspondent stowing away on a pirate vessel, can anybody tell us what she could have done differently? Aside from bragging on her employer, that is."

"She could have asked questions herself," Penelope said. "It's a reporter's job to ask questions, but it was obvious from the minute she started talking that she thought the job was to get onto their ship. Those two Hortens across from her were so inked up that she probably wouldn't have seen a skin reaction if they lied to her, but she might have at least tried to set some ground rules before leaving with them."

"Anybody else?" Thomas asked.

"I don't think she should have been trying to embed with pirates at all," a younger woman pointed out. "I mean, if you want to write a story about piracy, wouldn't it make more sense to travel with a merchant ship convoy and to get stories from the victims? Maybe one of the alien navies would let a reporter embed with them on an anti-piracy mission."

"I didn't understand what I read at the beginning, where my pirate said something about their mutual contact and finding a trustworthy crew," Bob said. "Did anybody go back and find out if the contact basically sold her to these guys?"

"Excellent question," Thomas said approvingly. "EarthCent Intelligence was asked to check into the circumstances, and we confirmed that Ms. Wysecki's contact was a spotter for the pirates, who openly boasted about the commission he received for delivering her."

"I've never been in the journalism business, but gathering information and cultivating sources for EarthCent Intelligence is about as close as you can get," Chance said. "I had a long talk with your publisher about the goal of this training course and we agreed on almost every point. Whatever story you're pursuing, there's always a bigger picture that you can't see, so it's crazy to stake your life on getting just one little bit of information in hopes of scoring a headline. Concentrate on figuring out what's going on and explaining it to your readers. That's what the subscribers want."

"But getting a scoop has always been the way to move ahead in our business," a man protested.

"Your editors and colleagues are holding meetings as we speak to establish new coverage guidelines," Chance reminded him. "The way your publisher explained it to me, the Galactic Free Press is trying to build a reputation for publishing useful news and getting it right. That means reporting on economic activity, shifts in political alliances that can affect trade, warnings about unsafe regions of space, and interviews with humans who have gone to interesting places and done interesting things. If people want excitement, they can get their adrenaline fix from the Grenouthians."

# Eleven

Dorothy arrived at the Open University exhibition hall expecting the usual formal affair, but it turned out that the calendars of several species were overlapping on the equivalent of a Friday night, so the students and attendees were in party mode. The theme of the exhibit was bar design, and all of the students whose work could potentially be applied to the universal concept of a place to get plastered were displaying their concept pieces. The fact that they were actually distributing drinks added to the celebratory atmosphere.

"Human?" inquired the Frunge girl at the entrance who was handing out empty metal cups.

"Yes," Dorothy said, accepting a cup. "We're not very rugged, gastronomically speaking."

"Try the Frunge ice tea," the girl suggested. "Just remind them to run it through the grub filter for you."

"Grub filter?"

"You know, the things that eat you from the inside out. Don't you get grubs?"

"Worms, maybe," Dorothy said, not wanting to make the girl feel bad.

"Just tell them to filter it. I saw a couple of Humans rush out of here earlier holding their stomachs."

Dorothy carefully avoided the Frunge ice tea maker on display, though she had to admit it made an intriguing presentation from a safe distance. A machine that looked like one of her father's old-fashioned compressors huffed away beneath the table, though the motor driving the belt looked like a dummy. She wondered if the concept was copied from human history, the same way she'd borrowed her hat design from the lost-and-found.

"Try sitting here," a Verlock rumbled as she passed, though the complete sentence didn't register until she was almost on to the next display. She turned around and returned to the hulking student, who was gesturing to a sturdy-looking stool with an equally beefy hand.

"It looks very strong," Dorothy replied slowly, having plenty of experience with Verlocks. She was surprised to see that the chair was cushioned, given the predilection of the leathery aliens for stone furniture, but when she hopped up onto the seat, a shock ran through her tailbone. An involuntary "Ouch," escaped her lips.

"Not good?" the Verlock forced out, looking concerned.

"The seat is harder than I expected," Dorothy prevaricated, but then she decided it was more important to give the designer her true reaction than to save his feelings. "Actually, it seems harder than stone, if that's possible."

"Thank you!" The Verlock looked about as joyous as Dorothy could ever recall seeing one of the normally stoic aliens. "Harder than it looks."

Dorothy just nodded and smiled, unsure if the Verlock was referring to the cushion itself or to the labor involved in creating anti-padding. She slid off the stool, rubbed her backside for a moment, and then moved on to the next table, where a Chert girl was waving her hands in the air like a magician.

"Human?" the Chert's assistant asked. "You're pretty enough to be Vergallian."

"Uh, thank you, I guess," Dorothy replied.

"I'm Tissent, and I'm helping my sister perform her bar concept," the Chert said, launching into a prepared speech. "Siffra has perfected a form of visual mixology based on hand movements. An array of light beams projected from between the glasses in the overhead rack is detected by sensors in the surface of the bar. This allows an experienced barkeep to mix and match from over one thousand bottles, down to amounts measured in hundreds of molecules. She's discovered exciting new mixed drinks by concentrating on the aesthetics of the blending motions rather than obsessing about ingredients. What can she make you?"

"Do you have any human bottles on tap?" Dorothy asked.

"Hang on a second," Tissent said, fiddling with something on his shoulder. Dorothy gasped as hundreds of bottles mounted in vertical racks suddenly appeared behind the bar. A thin transparent tube ran from each bottle to a manifold, and the outputs of a number of manifolds were combined into a crystal funnel, under which the Chert placed Dorothy's cup. Siffra had finished her last drink performance and waited expectantly for the human girl's order.

"I think I—no, the label is in Drazen," Dorothy said cautiously. "Those are all Vergallian with the square bottlenecks, I don't know what those are, or those. I'm sorry, but the only thing I recognize is the pink bottle there, reconstituted Florida grapefruit juice."

The Chert grimaced and muttered something to his sister. Her face fell, and she made a motion like a tomahawk chop through the light beams. The feeder lines all showed pink and the cup filled up with grapefruit juice.

A passing Horten turned to his companion and said, "What's the point of that? She moves her hand over the bar and the cup fills up with something. I could do it faster by grabbing the bottle."

The Chert student glowered at Dorothy for a brief moment, and then vanished as her brother handed the ambassador's daughter the cup of juice.

"Oh, look what you've done," Tissent scolded the human. "I only got her to turn off her invisibility projector a few minutes ago. The whole visual concept doesn't work if people can't see her moving her arms."

"Can she mix drinks if she's invisible?" Dorothy couldn't help asking.

"Of course," the Chert replied. "She's not really invisible, you know. You just can't see her because her projector is feeding your eyes false images. It doesn't trick the light beams." He turned away from the ambassador's daughter and began pleading with the empty space. "Come on, Siffra. Everybody loved it. You can't go by what a couple of Hortens think just because the Human doesn't know how to order a drink."

"Hey, Dorothy," Chance said, approaching the table. "Is she playing a Sharf mixology organ? I don't really care about the taste as long as it burns, but I like to watch."

"You can see her?" the Chert's brother inquired.

"I'm an artificial so my frame rate is way higher than you biologicals," Chance replied immodestly. "How about something strong? You pick it."

"Did you hear that, Siffra?" Tissent said. "I'll bet she'd like to watch a Slice and Dice."

"Wow!" Chance said, as drops of liquid began to fall into the fresh cup. "She's really great. I shouldn't have compared your device to a Sharf mixology organ. This is much better."

Siffra flickered back into existence, and Chance gave Dorothy a wink as the Chert student waved her hands through the air like a mad orchestra conductor. A group of people gathered to watch, and as near as Dorothy could tell, the mixologist was pulling just a drop or two out of each bottle. Finally, she stopped moving and nodded to her brother. He brought out a small lighter and lit the drink, which burned with a translucent blue flame.

Chance accepted the cup and tossed back the concoction, smacking her lips. The spectators applauded and began calling out drink orders to the Chert girl, whose invisibility projector remained inactive. Her brother nodded his thanks to Chance as the artificial person drew Dorothy away.

"I've never seen you at one of the Open University student exhibitions before," the ambassador's daughter said. "Are you thinking about taking a course?"

"Moi?" Chance replied with an exaggerated French accent, putting her hand on her chest. "I came because Thomas dragged me, though I ditched him for fun a few minutes ago. He says it's important we keep up with the latest in bar design concepts for professional reasons. Where's your man?"

"David's working. I have to come to these exhibitions as part of my Open University design program."

"You see? I told you school is a drag on creativity," Chance said, guiding Dorothy past a display of iron-banded bottles suspended in a magnetic field for no apparent purpose. "Oh, there's Thomas. Let's go this way."

The artificial person pulled Dorothy into a curtained-off section of the exhibition hall, where the lighting was so dim that the girl could barely make out the hand in front of her face.

"I can't see a thing," she complained.

"Your eyes will adjust in a minute. The Grenouthians prefer their bars to be very dark because it reminds them of burrows or something. Do you think Thomas saw us?"

"Why are you ducking him?"

"Practice. The training camp has been so busy lately that I rarely get a chance to go out on real missions, and Thomas has practically given up ever getting back into the field. How can we maintain our edge if all we do is run around Mac's Bones all day?"

"I don't know," Dorothy replied. "I mean, it's not like Dad and Woojin have to go back to being mercenaries to teach self-defense."

"Have your eyes adjusted? It's starting."

Dorothy peered around in the dark, trying to see what Chance was talking about, and she finally spotted what looked like silvery bubbles rising inside of a transparent cylinder. The illumination level increased in small but discrete increments, as if somebody were turning a mechanical switch with a hundred detents, and the barely visible audience began to make appreciative noises. Dorothy realized that there were a number of the bubbling columns in the curtained-off area which had initially been blocked from view by the other guests.

"I don't get it," Dorothy whispered to Chance. "What's the big deal about putting bubble lights in a bar?"

"They aren't just lights," the artificial person said in her normal register. "Can't you see the taps at the bottom?"

"They're lighting fixtures and they're giant bottles?"

"More like light-kegs I'd say," Chance replied. "The Grenouthians did a documentary on Earth breweries a few cycles ago that wasn't entirely insulting. We all watched it with your dad after training camp one day. I'll bet these students have figured out a way to brew an intoxicant in the style of human beer that works on Grenouthians. The light show is just a way to market it to bunnies who aren't used to bubbly drinks."

"But the Grenouthians have been around almost as long as the Verlocks, millions of years," Dorothy said. "They're always going on about how they don't have anything to learn from us. How can something like beer be new to them?"

"You take it for granted because you grew up with your father home-brewing on the lower deck of your home," Chastity explained. She had to raise her voice to talk over the enthusiastic response of the bunnies who were quaffing samples of brew from the light columns. "Let's get going. Thomas must have passed by now."

"We're coming with you," said a voice at Dorothy's side. She turned to see the Vergallian couple from the artist's party which Tinka had attended with the painful poet. "I wondered if I would run into you again," the woman continued. "I'm Affie and this is Stick."

"I'm Dorothy and this is Chance," the ambassador's daughter replied, though she couldn't help wondering when Vergallians had become so friendly. Then she caught a telltale whiff of Kraaken stick and guessed that the name that the male went under wasn't the same one his parents had given him at birth. "Are you both students?"

"I am," Affie replied as they emerged from the Grenouthian area back onto the main exhibition floor. "Stick just hangs around bothering me and doing a little business. Come on. A bunch of us are meeting in the Drazen lounge."

125

Dorothy turned to check with Chance, but the artificial person was crouching behind a Verlock, making a face and pointing back towards the entrance. The ambassador's daughter looked around and saw that Thomas was headed directly for them. Turning to tell Chance that she'd probably been spotted would certainly have given away her position, so Dorothy settled for muttering, "I think the jig is up," out of the corner of her mouth, and tried to look casual as she fell in beside Affie.

"So what are you studying?" the Vergallian woman asked.

"I'm into fashion and clothing design. I wanted to start a business with my Gem friend, but she went back to their homeworld to sleep until they grow a male clone for her."

"You're so lucky. I never had a clone friend and we didn't get any aliens visiting our settlement. I never thought I'd convince my family to let me study on a station, but then my oldest sister had triplets, all girls, so now I'm far enough down the succession line to be free of it all. I always wanted to visit the tunnel network."

"So you're not from the Empire of a Hundred Worlds," Dorothy remarked. "I wondered why you were so different from the upper caste Vergallians I've met."

"I'm from fleet, though my family are planet-side now. We never went along with that tech-ban craziness that the Empire uses to maintain the status quo. My presentation piece to get accepted in the Open University sculpture program depicted a dying mercenary slashing at a battle cruiser with a sword."

"Except she does abstract," Stick interjected. "It looks like two melted blobs connected by a cube."

"That sounds very interesting," Dorothy said politely.

"Anyway, I came at a good time," Affie continued. "Nothing much happens on the stations for a hundred thousand years or so, and then some new species comes along and shakes things up for a while. You always see it first in the visual arts. Sculpture is like the radiation detector in the core."

"The canary in the coal mine," Dorothy surmised.

"A little bird underground?" The Vergallian girl frowned, trying to make sense of what her translation implant had fed her. "Oh, I get it. A low-tech poison gas detector. Hey, should we light a stinker before we go in, Stick?"

The Vergallian male lived up to his name by pulling a stick of Kraaken Red out of his vest and lighting the end. Then he blew on it, putting out the flame but causing the ember to glow brightly. When he stopped blowing, it began to smoke. He held it under his nose, inhaled, and passed the stick to Dorothy.

"Go ahead," Affie said. "It's perfectly safe for Humans. Besides, you won't want to touch any of the drinks in the Drazen lounge. It's a good thing you brought your own because their idea of a stiff drink would eat through your stomach lining."

Dorothy hesitated, but not wanting to come across like an innocent kid, she waved a little of the smoke under her nose and inhaled. The drug took effect immediately, and when she tried to pass the stick to Affie, she ended up offering it to the empty space between the two Vergallians.

"Uh, oh. I didn't think anybody could have a worse head for the stuff than you, Affie," Stick observed.

"Don't pay attention to him," the Vergallian girl told Dorothy, taking the Kraaken stick from her hand, then on second thought, relieving the girl of her drink as well and giving it to Stick to carry. "He's just jealous of the fact that we can catch flight without burning a handful of the things. Come on."

Dorothy might have stood paralyzed or perhaps sat down on the floor if Affie hadn't grabbed her arm and towed her into the Drazen exhibit area. Several students had pooled their resources to create a concept lounge which looked like it had been copied from a human bar as depicted in pre-immersive films. The main features were a high bar with the bottles displayed on shallow shelves. Strategically placed mirrors and candles maximized the allure of the liquids, and the picture was completed by a bank of taps, the handles displaying human brands of beer that were no longer available on Earth, much less the station. For some reason, the students and their guests seem to find the décor irresistible.

"I don't get it," Dorothy said, struggling against the numbness of her tongue. "This is just a copy of a human bar." Sweeping her arm to illustrate the scope of her disdain, she knocked over a glass on the table they were passing. Fortunately, it was a sweet drink rather than a Divverflip, or somebody might have gotten hurt.

"Easy, Dorry," the Vergallian girl said, tightening her grip on Dorothy's other arm. "Let's just find a table with some open chairs." As she spoke, she gave her companion a sharp look. The Vergallian male moved ahead of them and bribed a trio of Drazen students to abandon their table in return for a pair of Kraaken sticks.

Dorothy might have missed the transition from standing to sitting if not for the fact that everybody else in the room suddenly got taller. "Hey," she said weakly, but then her eyes fell on the guttering candle in a colored glass globe that had been placed in the center of the table. No matter how she concentrated, she couldn't get the little flame to stop dancing about, leading her to repeat, "Hey," in protest.

"Drink some of your juice," Affie said, retrieving the grapefruit juice from Stick and placing it on the table in front of Dorothy. The ambassador's daughter stopped staring at the candle and started staring at the cup. The Vergallian girl sighed and lifted the cup to the human's mouth, carefully pouring a bit of juice between her lips. Dorothy struggled to remember something that she was forgetting, and just before the juice began to dribble out, it occurred to her to swallow.

"That's better," Stick said. "I was afraid you were going to zone out on us for a minute there. Good stuff, huh?"

"Mmm," Dorothy replied.

"It's important to try new things with new sentients," Affie said, launching into her favorite topic. "That's why the arrival of a new species on the galactic stage always shakes things up. Humans are like catalysts."

"Cat lists," Dorothy agreed.

"I didn't choose the Open University campus on Union Station at random, you know. I studied up first, and this place has been the nexus of activity on the tunnel network for the last two decades."

"Nexus. Next us," Dorothy pronounced, feeling that she had unraveled one of the mysteries of the multiverse.

Affie waited politely for a moment to see if her new friend wanted to elucidate the point, and then continued. "Do you know that Union Station is the only place in the galaxy where little Stryx go to school with young biologicals, and it only started around twenty years ago?"

"Metoo," Dorothy confirmed.

129

"And the whole business with the Kasilians giving away all their stuff and turning back from species suicide. Do you think something like that comes along every day? And then, before you know it, the Gem revolution gets its start here."

"Mist," Dorothy concurred.

"I missed something? Do you mean that stupid Verlock game everybody was playing for a while? Fads like that happen all the time, though come to think of it, I guess Raider/Trader was kind of major. Anyway, when I heard the Wanderers came through, I was like, there's just something going on at that place. Then your Stryx librarian opened a theme park, and I told my parents that this is where I wanted to finish my education."

"Libbyland? So tired," Dorothy said, struggling to keep her head up.

"And what happens next? The Emperor of the Cayl decides to dissolve their seven-million-year-old empire, only after spending a few weeks on Union Station, he changes his mind and everything goes back to normal. I got here during the open house and I couldn't believe how the Stryx let those aliens run amok. But I never would have gotten to see the Cayl and their dogs otherwise. I did a piece depicting a warrior and his hound."

"It looks like two melted blobs connected by a cube," Stick affirmed.

"Blobs," Dorothy murmured. Then she put her head on the table and fell asleep.

# Twelve

As the assistant producer counted "Let's Make Friends" back in from the second commercial break, Aisha looked over to make sure that EarthCent's president hadn't wandered away from his mark. In the week since the president and his mistress came to stay in the ice harvester, Aisha had concluded that the titular leader of humanity suffered from an attention disorder. Fortunately, Hildy had come along to keep him on his toes. The instrumental version of the show's theme song began to play, and the red "live" on the front immersive camera came on.

"Is everybody ready to meet today's special guest?" Aisha asked the cast.

"Yes," the children chorused in their own languages. The Grenouthian studio dubbed the show for all broadcast audiences in real time so that watchers didn't require translation implants. The children were all equipped with an in-ear feed for their own language.

"The man we're about to meet is the president of EarthCent, which employs the human ambassadors on Stryx stations," Aisha said. She regretted the convoluted explanation, but given the limited jurisdiction and authority of EarthCent, it was the best she could do. Most of the children nodded, willing to take her word for it, but the little Horten girl raised a tentative hand.

"Yes, Noninth?" Aisha asked.

"My mother is an entertainment consultant for the Horten embassy, and she says that the Human ambassadors work for the Stryx."

"Well, that's one way to look at it," Aisha acknowledged. "Because we humans are new to the tunnel network, the Stryx pay most of the bills for EarthCent. But the ambassadors work for the president, sort of."

"So the president works for the Stryx and the ambassadors don't know?" Noninth followed up.

"Why don't we invite him on and then you can ask him yourself?" Aisha suggested. She missed having Blythe's son on the show, since Jonah could instantly come up with an explanation for any question posed about humanity without worrying about accuracy. Unfortunately, he had aged off the cast.

The children all turned toward the waiting president and chanted, "Let's Make Friends, Mr. EarthCent President."

"Thank you, children," the president replied, approaching center stage with a bouncy step. "Please call me Stephen. May I ask your names?"

"I'm Cudge," declared the not-so-little Dollnick girl. "And I'm hungry."

"Tump," said the little Drazen boy.

"Noninth," the Horten girl said. "Do you really work for the Stryx?"

"It depends who you ask," the president responded diplomatically. "And who's that next to you?"

"Thyntorial," the young Verlock rumbled.

"Fajav," squeaked a shy-looking shrub.

"At least part your hair vines a little so he can get a peek at you," Aisha admonished the little Frunge girl. Fajav complied for about two seconds before covering her face again.

"And I'm Harry," announced a six-year-old boy. "My parents met at your dance."

"My dance?" the president responded, looking questioningly at Aisha.

"The monthly EarthCent mixer," the host explained. "The embassy manager runs it."

"Then I'm happy to take credit and glad to be of service," Stephen told the boy.

"I'm the youngest," said the last child, a pure-white bunny whose parents both worked on the show. Fortunately, the president remembered from his ambassadorial days that the Grenouthians rarely shared their names with outsiders, so he didn't pursue the matter.

"I'm very happy to be here on 'Let's Make Friends,' and I hope you'll all treat me just like a kid who happens to be big," Stephen said. "I'm looking forward to playing games and telling stories, and I also brought Aisha a present. Should I give it to her now or later?"

The children replied with a contradictory chorus, so the president pointed at each child in turn.

"Now," said the Horten.

"Later," declared the Dollnick.

"Later," said the human boy.

"Now," piped the Grenouthian.

"Later," squeaked the Frunge girl.

"Now," the Verlock said.

"Later," was the Drazen boy's response.

"That's four to three, so I'll give it to her later," the president said agreeably. "So, Noninth," he continued, turning to the little Horten girl. "All of you just made a decision for me, so am I still working for the Stryx?"

The Horten girl looked puzzled. "Maybe you work for the Stryx part-time."

"Higher Determinism," the young Verlock mathematician rumbled, but everybody ignored him.

"Do you ever have young Stryx on your show?" the president asked Aisha.

"Not yet," Aisha replied. She swallowed her annoyance at the president for going off script so quickly since she couldn't help being impressed that he came up with the obvious question that nobody else had ever asked. "Do you have a human game to share with the children?"

The president hesitated for a moment. He had rehearsed this part of the show with Aisha and Hildy and they had come up with a variation on the telephone game. The idea was that the little aliens would sit in a circle, remove their in-ear translation devices, and whisper a repeated word to see how badly it got distorted. But looking at the cute little aliens, the president had another idea.

"I always like playing the 'One Of These,' game," he replied. "Everybody sit in a circle and I'll teach you."

Sitting in a circle was the most common arrangement on the show, and in a matter of seconds, all seven of the children were seated on the carpet, more or less evenly spaced. Aisha would usually sit with a child on each side, but something about the name of the president's unplanned game made her nervous, so she sat cross-legged next to him.

"Great," the president continued. "It's a simple game, really. "You say, 'I have one of these,' and then you touch different parts of your body. Then the player on your right says, 'I have one of these,' and starts with the third part the last player touched. So if the third thing I touch is my ear,

134

Harry, who is on my right, would have to touch his ear first or he's out. When somebody goes out, the next person starts fresh. Get it?"

A feeling of dread overtook Aisha as she thought of myriad ways the president's touching game could go wrong, but the feed went out live on the Grenouthian network so it was already too late. At least the children were too young to try to embarrass each other on purpose.

"I'll start," the president said, and turned to Harry. "I have one of these." Then he rapidly touched his own knee, his left elbow, his nose, and his ear.

"I have one of these," the boy said immediately, and correctly touched his nose. He turned to the Verlock boy sitting next to him and repeated the key phrase, "I have one of these." Then he rapidly touched his nose, mouth, his nose again, his left ear, his right ear, his nose again, and the top of his head. Thyntorial gaped at the human.

"I think you might have gone a bit fast for our Verlock friend," Aisha hastened to say. "Perhaps we could try a different game?"

"I have one of these," the Verlock grated out, and touched his left ear. Then he slowly began turning to the young bunny next to him.

"You're out," Harry said. "I touched my nose third."

"You touched your nose first," the Verlock replied slowly. "Doesn't count the second time."

"Is that how Verlocks play this game?" the president asked. "I don't have that rule."

"Now I'm out," Thyntorial rumbled.

"So it's your turn to start, Youngest," Stephen addressed the Grenouthian child.

"I have one of these," the bunny said, touching each ear in turn, and then putting a finger in his abdominal pouch.

"I don't have one of those," the Horten girl said in dismay.

"You're out," the other children chorused. Noninth looked pleadingly at Aisha, but the host shook her head sadly.

"I have one of these," the Drazen boy who was next in the circle declared. He touched his nose, his ear, and then grabbed his tentacle.

"No fair!" the Frunge girl cried. "Nobody else has a tentacle."

"You're out," the children chorused, enjoying the novelty of the game. The Horten girl who had already been knocked out seemed to take great satisfaction in the elimination of the Frunge.

"I have one of these," the Dollnick girl announced with a broad smile. She used one of her upper arms to touch her nose, her ear, and each of her lower arms in turn.

"I'm afraid I only have two arms," Aisha said. "But I..."

"You're out!" the children all shouted, drowning out the rest of her words.

"Cheer up," the president said to Aisha. "I just counted ahead, and unless Harry gets the Grenouthian out, I'll be the one short a set of arms next round."

"You're all out," the assistant director called. "We're on commercial break. The booth says we have to move on to Storytellers when we get back because it's already in the network's synopsis for today's show."

Aisha smiled with relief. "Did you hear that, children? The director says we have to start Storytellers or all of our watchers will be disappointed."

"That's not fair to Stephen," Tump protested. It wasn't often that he got a chance to show off his tentacle on the show, and after counting ahead, he was sure he could eliminate at least one more of the cast. "We didn't finish playing his game."

The children divided into two arguing camps over the injustice of the programming change, the composition of the sides depending on whether or not they had already been forced out of the game by lack of a physical attribute.

"It's too bad we're on commercial break," the president said to Aisha. "The children are providing a perfect example of how species form alliances based on their competing interests."

"I think that's a bit advanced for the six-year-old demographic," Aisha replied. She had a policy of letting the children guide the show, and now she was at a loss for how to convince them to agree on abandoning the game midway.

The president suggested a solution. "How about we play Storytellers and I lead?"

"You know Storytellers?" Aisha asked in surprise.

"I do my homework," the president replied confidently.

Before the host could quiz the president on his intentions, the assistant director counted them back in and the cameras went live.

"We ran out of time to show the rest of the 'I have one of these,' game, so our special guest is going to lead in today's Storytellers. Stephen?"

"Once upon..." the president began.

"A TIME!" the children all shouted.

"The planet Earth couldn't catch up with the advanced species and the children were all sad. The president of EarthCent came to Union Station to ask for help from our alien friends so we could have a better future. First the president went to the Dollnicks and he asked how they could help." Here the president stopped and pointed at Cudge.

The Dollnick girl replied without hesitating. "The smart Dollnicks taught the Humans about terraforming and colony ships, so they could make new places to live."

"Thank you," the president said. "After the Dollnicks taught the humans terraforming for a fair price, the Grenouthians arrived." He stopped and pointed at the bunny.

"And we—," the young bunny paused and thought for a moment. "And the Grenouthians taught the Humans how to make shows that everybody likes."

"That's right," Stephen said encouragingly. "The Grenouthians lead the galaxy in news and entertainment. But we humans don't have the math to understand holograms and colony ships, and our science says the tunnel network can't exist." The president nodded to Thyntorial.

"The Verlocks built Earth a math academy," the Verlock boy said slowly. "And a magic school."

"Now we're cooking," Stephen said enthusiastically. "But the humans were so far behind that the biggest businesses on Earth could only export simple things, like food, silicon crystals and carbon nanotubes." The children all giggled, and the president pointed to the Drazen boy.

"So the Drazens taught the Humans to make new things to sell without getting their planet all dirty," Tump said excitedly.

"Exactly what we need," the president said. "But the traders from Earth could only afford to buy old Sharf ships with money borrowed from the Stryx because we don't build our own."

"The Hortens can teach you," Noninth offered generously. "We build lots of small ships. My brother says ours are the best kind for trading."

Aisha looked on in amazement as the president led the children through a happy tale about Earth's future. She had come to dread the Storytellers segment herself, because the communal plot development invariably led to monsters who ate little children, or witches who turned them into other aliens that their parents didn't like. Not surprisingly, it was one of the most anticipated segments each week.

"But do you know which species already owns a lot of land on Earth?" the president asked. The little children all shook their heads. "The Frunge. The Frunge traded a wealthy human a planet for money to buy some large forests."

"And the Frunge came and taught people to be nicer to trees," Fajav said from behind her hair vines.

"And how did the humans treat all of the aliens who came to help them?" the president asked Harry.

"We gave them all ice cream," the little boy declared. "And Sheezle bugs, and fertilizer, and giant carrots."

"Sheezle bugs?" Cudge asked hopefully.

"Lots of Sheezle bugs," the boy asserted.

The Dollnick girl's stomach began to rumble audibly, and thankfully a commercial break intervened.

"Did you skip lunch today?" Aisha asked the girl.

"Breakfast," Cudge replied sadly. "Why do you keep changing the show time?"

"The time is always the same for me," Aisha replied. "It's human time. Your parents live on Dollnick time, so it's difficult for you. This is the last commercial break, so we

only have a little more to go and then you can get something to eat."

"Will I have time to give you the award?" the president
asked Aisha.

"Can you keep politics out of it?" Aisha pleaded. "I
don't know how the producers are going to react to the
fairy tale you turned into a campaign for the betterment of
Earth."

The assistant director thumped his furry foot to get
their attention, and then counted the show back in.

"I think we have just enough time for Stephen to give
me something he brought all the way from Earth," Aisha
said self-consciously. She always tried to make the children
the center of attention and she hoped the president would
keep it short.

"EarthCent has created a special medal to thank Aisha
for her show," the president said. He turned to where
Hildy stood in the wings, but she shook her head and
pantomimed an action by sliding her hand down the
outside of her hip. "And I have that medal right here," he
continued, reaching in his pocket and tugging on a loop of
blue ribbon. The ribbon pulled taut, and then the heavy
bronze medallion which had barely fit in his pocket
popped out.

"What's it for?" Noninth asked.

"To thank Aisha for creating this show," the president
replied patiently.

"She means, what does it do?" the Drazen boy asserted.

"Oh. I can hang it around her neck with this ribbon,"
the president said, putting his words into action.

"Is it a shield to stop arrows?" the Dollnick girl asked.
"It's awfully small."

"It doesn't look like her," the Frunge girl commented, peering out from her veil of hair vines.

"That's funny, I thought it wasn't a bad likeness," the president said.

"The Surprise Day Aisha is much better," the Horten girl declared, and the other children chimed in with their agreement.

"What's a Surprise Day Aisha?" the president asked, turning to the host.

Aisha sighed, and retrieved the Dollnick Tan tuber from its place of honor on the mantle of the cozy set.

The president took the tuber in one hand, squinted at the medal he had just presented, and asked, "Could I borrow the potato for a mold? We'll have your medal recast."

"I want to see it again," Harry said.

"Me too," the other children chimed in, so the president passed the tuber to the boy, and the children jostled each other for another look.

The assistant director caught Aisha's eye and made the wrapping-up movement.

"Let's show our new friend how we sing together," Aisha said brightly.

The children dutifully formed their double-ranked chorus line, with the taller cast members in the back. As the music began playing, they launched into the show's theme song.

*Don't be a stranger because I look funny,*
*You look weird to me, but let's make friends.*
*I'll give you a tissue if your nose is runny,*
*I'm as scared as you, so let's make friends.*

141

"That's a wrap," the assistant director called. "They want to see you in the booth, Mrs. McAllister. Good luck."

"Oh, I'll see you tomorrow, children." Aisha managed a weak smile at Hildy, who had come onto the set as soon as the immersive cameras went cold. Then the host headed up to the booth to face the music.

"I think that went pretty well," the president said to his public relations director. "I just hope that the parents watching with their children don't judge us by the relief of Aisha on the medallion, since that potato put it to shame."

"I couldn't see it that well from where I was standing," Hildy said. "Where is it?"

The president looked around the set where the parents were gathering their children. A towering Dollnick was carrying away his daughter, who munched happily on a Tan tuber.

"Never mind," the president said. "I don't think that potato will be a problem in the future."

# Thirteen

"So you aren't going to assign reporters to cover piracy anymore?" Penelope asked. "It seems like kind of an important news item to be ignoring."

"We aren't prohibiting correspondents from reporting on lost ships or the impact of piracy in their zones of coverage," Walter replied patiently. "The majority of our reporters will be assigned to worlds with large populations of human laborers or sectors where humans trade and travel. What we're halting is the practice of sending correspondents to the frontiers of the tunnel network for the sake of reporting on piracy."

"How about war coverage?" another correspondent asked. "My series about the succession wars on Hwoult Five won an award from the mercenary guild for best coverage on Vergallian tech-ban worlds last year."

"We're still discussing where to draw the line on that, but we'll want at least episodic coverage wherever there's a significant presence of human mercenaries," Daggert replied. "I find that I've been shanghaied into accepting a new position as the roving conflict editor, so you war junkies will be reporting to me from now on."

"Follow-up question," the correspondent stated, bringing a laugh from the reporters gathered in the newsroom of the Galactic Free Press. "What's a significant presence?"

"That's the part we haven't settled on yet, but barring special circumstances, we're talking about something like regiment or brigade strength, say a couple thousand guys. There are plenty of Vergallian royals who keep a few human infantry or cavalry troops on the payroll, but they serve more as ceremonial guards than strategic assets."

"How about off-network wars?" another correspondent asked.

"Nix," Daggert said. "We're restricting off-network coverage to special assignments on topics with a direct impact on humanity. As long as we're under Stryx protection, which aliens are killing which other aliens halfway across the galaxy just doesn't rate as news our readers can use."

"But that was my suggestion box entry for the new slogan and you didn't give me credit," Bob Steelforth protested indignantly. "News our readers can use."

"I'm afraid it's not original," Chastity told the young reporter with a smile. "I did a historical check with Libby, and it appears that over eighty percent of newspapers ever published on Earth employed some variation of 'News you can use,' for a motto at one point or another. We're going to give it a try, so my apologies to those of you who independently came up with, 'All the news that's fit to print.' And whoever submitted, 'If it bleeds, it leads,' you might want to check if the Grenouthians have any job openings."

"Katy Hicks," the Dollnick ag worlds correspondent identified herself. "So we're going to focus on business and sports from now on?"

"All the news our readers can use," Walter repeated. "I had a chance to talk to EarthCent's top public relations expert at the president's reception, and she suggested simply surveying our readers about where they feel our coverage is lacking. We did that in yesterday's issue, and I

144

have to admit that the results came as something of a surprise."

"Not enough sports coverage, right?" a reporter called out.

"That was on the list, but fourth down," the managing editor replied. "The number one complaint was our lack of a 'Home' section. Readers living on alien worlds want to see more recipes, shopping tips and consumer advice, how to incorporate alien technologies into their daily lives. Basically, they're less interested in news than they are in practical help for living."

"What was the second most popular request?" Katy asked.

"An improved personals section and relationship advice," Chastity answered. "We're going to establish a number of advice columns with permanent bylines, so if any of you are experts on broken hearts or angry teenagers, feel free to try out for the positions."

"But we aren't going to start publishing personals," Walter said. "There are plenty of other places people can go for that already, and there was a turf conflict with our back-office support in any case. The third request is the one that surprised me the most, which was more coverage of Earth."

"Really?" several voices asked at once.

"It may have to do with all the press we've been giving the president's visit, but most people still have family back on Earth and it turns out there's more interest than we thought," Chastity confirmed. "It's a minority, but they were very passionate about it."

"How do you know?" Bob said.

"The survey form asked readers to rate their top five coverage requests in order of importance. Only one in four readers mentioned Earth, but most of them put it at the top of the list. Maybe some of them are planning on retiring there, maybe it's just nostalgia, but we're negotiating with several Earth news syndicates to exchange stories on a one-for-one basis. If you knew what they wanted to charge for full syndication rights, you'd all run screaming from the room."

"If sports came in fourth, what was fifth?" somebody called out.

"It wasn't important," Walter said. "Now what we'd..."

"Go ahead and tell them," Daggert interrupted him. "We've just pulled the rug out from under some of our best correspondents so the least we can do is be honest."

"It was just something about the crossword puzzle," Walter muttered irritably.

"Are we cancelling it?" a reporter in the back asked, sounding hopeful. "That thing drives me nuts."

"The readers love my weekly crossword puzzle. They would just like to see the work of a guest cruciverbalist from time to time."

"That's your problem in a nutshell," the same reporter said, snorting in disgust. "Cruciverbalist. You keep using words I've never heard of, and I write for a living. Why not do a puzzle that only uses vocabulary from our published stories?"

"Crossword puzzles aren't supposed to be easy," Walter retorted. "They're supposed to challenge you, to leave you gnashing your teeth in frustration. Most cruciverbalists feel they have to choose between offering cryptic clues or demanding arcane knowledge. I try to combine the two by tying the clues into the puzzle title."

"But they don't make any sense," another correspondent complained. "Every week, I get through almost the

146

whole puzzle except for a missing word here and there. Then when the solution is published, I find out that half of my answers were wrong, even though they meshed together perfectly. It's like you're intentionally choosing ambiguous clues to lead me down the garden path."

"And what's with all the extinct animals?" Penelope piled on. "In the middle of a puzzle about the history of transportation titled, 'Night Moves,' you had 'Ectocion' and 'Eohippus.' When I got back to a Stryx station and asked the librarian for help, he said they were dog-sized creatures from fifty million years ago."

"At least they maybe, just maybe, evolved into horses," said the reporter who had first objected to the crossword puzzles. "That same puzzle was full of prehistoric plants that all ended in 'oideae.' There were as many black squares as open spaces because he couldn't come up with crossing words."

"The horsey things had to eat something," Walter defended himself. "If you think you can do better, go ahead and submit a puzzle."

"Will we get authorship credit?" the reporter asked.

"I had an idea about that," Chastity said. "Why not save the bottom-right across space for your name or initials? I think it would be fun."

"You don't even do the puzzles," Walter chastised the owner and publisher.

"Maybe I'll start," Chastity retorted. "Shall we move on to our main business for the day?"

"My feelings exactly," Walter agreed huffily. "The most important editorial change we're planning didn't make the top five request list, though many of our readers mentioned it when we asked for general comments. We want to leverage our ongoing coverage of the president's visit to step up our reporting on nascent human political movements throughout the galaxy."

"Why?" Katy asked. "What does it matter to my readers on Dollnick ag planets what some demagogue on a Drazen open world has to say, much less what politicians are arguing about back on Earth?"

"Politics may seem like a luxury to contract laborers who are living on alien worlds, but we want to report on new political movements before they grow into governments. Otherwise, potential candidates who don't happen to be on the spot with good timing or know the right people will be left out of the process."

"But reporting on politicians will create a self-fulfilling prophecy," Penelope objected. "You'll be putting our correspondents in the position of king-makers, since the people we choose to write about in the paper will be turned into public figures through our efforts. Even if the articles are critical, they'll have the effect of lending the paper's credibility to the subjects."

"And we've anticipated that problem, which is why we intend to adopt a version of Horten rules for our coverage," Chastity said.

"Horten rules?" Bob asked, looking bewildered. "But I've been studying up on the governing systems of the tunnel species through the Open University extension program, and I still don't understand how the Hortens run their worlds. The Vergallians and the Dollnicks have a form of royalty, the Frunge have bizarre elections, the Drazens have singing competitions and the Grenouthians and Verlocks use civil service tests. The only thing I understood about the Horten system is that it involves their military."

"We aren't talking about adopting their system of fighting simulated wars to select leaders," Chastity explained. "It's how their press covers the fleet officers and reservists who are eligible to stand for executive positions. It's not some free-for-all where anybody can get into the fight. They have a selection process for the candidates at every command level, which isn't so unlike the old Earth campaigns. It's a multi-party system that produces cohesive governments, since the war simulations can't end in a draw."

"I don't get it."

"The Hortens have political parties, think of them as sides in a multi-party war, which each have their own group of supporters. Every election cycle, the supporters outfit a virtual fleet and elect members to man the ships. All of the ships, well, think of them as game pieces, must be purchased from the Horten election commission, which uses the money to pay for the government which is eventually installed. The new government serves until the money runs out."

"That's crazy," Penelope said. "They sell the government to the highest bidder?"

"It doesn't work that way, though what you've described is a fair approximation of how the Frunge operate. After the Horten political parties field their fleets, the largest of which represent tens of billions of citizens, the smaller parties can make alliances to perform as auxiliaries. Or, they can choose to arrive late at the battle and hope that the large fleets will decimate each other, giving survivors an opportunity to pick up the pieces. The elective government positions are eventually staffed by the best-performing members of the winning fleet or coalition."

"So the admiral doesn't automatically become Grand Leader?"

"Right. They use a complex scoring system that makes it statistically possible for any member of the winning fleet to qualify, though the odds certainly favor those in command positions. And like all advanced species, most government functions are run by career civil servants, so the leadership changes have limited impact."

"So what's so special about the way their press covers the fighting, or the simulated fighting?" Bob persisted in asking.

"It's not about the fighting at all, though they do cover that when the battle occurs. It's about how the candidates present themselves to the paid-up party members who elect them to their positions for the fleets. All of the officer ranks stand for election, and since nobody knows how they will end up in the scoring if their side triumphs, the candidates, in essence, don't know what positions they're running for."

"Good grief," somebody muttered.

"It makes a lot of sense if you think about it," Chastity said. "The Hortens aren't looking for politicians who will turn their system upside-down or rush them off to war. They just want leaders with, well, leadership ability. So their press apportions coverage according to the rank of the candidate, but they also create an election book each year that gives an up-to-date biography of all of the candidates in each party. The voters concentrate on who they want to select from their own party since they have no say over who the other parties will select in any case."

"I still don't get it," Bob said.

"I'm not entirely convinced it's such a great scheme myself," Walter admitted. "But I do like the idea of press coverage focusing on a living biography of each candidate, rather than reporting on every speech or trying to control the process with gotcha questions. I haven't spent as much time looking into Horten politics as our publisher, but from what I can see, they end up electing technocrats rather than actors."

"What's wrong with actors?" a reporter demanded.

"I didn't mean to denigrate the thespian profession," Walter said, eliciting a groan from the reporter who had complained about the crossword puzzle vocabulary. "I meant it in the sense of individuals who can win support based on their performance skills and appearance. The Horten coverage concentrates on researching and analyzing candidate biographies, including full financial disclosure, work history, military and academic records. So the voters choose candidates based on their past performance, and the simulated battle selects the group who are best at working together with the resources they have. It also helps eliminate the older figure-head candidates who no longer perform at a high level."

"In any case, we want to start creating an election book for humans," Chastity said, cutting short the debate. "I'm sure most of you already keep notes on all of the public figures on your beats, so the first phase is simply to formalize that process and create a central database. We don't expect you to drop everything to work on this."

"So you want us to write biographies of promising public individuals?" Penelope asked.

"We designed a standard form, starting with the same template as the Horten election commission biographies, and then we brought in some experts to tweak it for humanity," Chastity continued. "It's almost a shame that we can't read each other's emotions through changes in

151

skin color like the Hortens, but they do say that losing the ability to lie almost destroyed them."

"It can't hurt to have the basics on file for business leaders, sports figures, entertainers and famous people in general," Walter added. "Politicians have to start somewhere, and being known is a serious advantage. We're also planning an expanded obituary section, so having the data ready to go is a big help."

"Doesn't EarthCent Intelligence have all this information already?" a voice called out.

"They're focused on aliens," Chastity replied. "As far as I know, the only humans they try to keep tabs on are their agents."

"And it's all going to be public record?" another reporter asked. "Anybody who wants to access this information will be able to get it?"

"Only if they have a full Galactic Free Press subscription," Walter said. "When humans start holding more elections, we'll release any relevant information we have on the candidates standing for office as a free guide. But you have to remember that the back office services provided by the Stryx cost money, so we aren't going to turn the newspaper's database into a 24/7 resource for anybody who feels like checking up on their neighbors."

"Not to mention marketers," Chastity added.

"The station librarian is rolling out the new form to your reporter tabs as we speak," Walter said. "Next time you power up your tab and connect to Stryxnet it should be there."

All around the room, reporters whipped out their tabs and checked for updates.

"Finding your ideal match?" Katy asked incredulously. "I thought you said we aren't getting into the personals business."

"Libby?" Chastity called out in annoyance. "Did you outsource the conversion job?"

"I asked Jeeves to take care of it," the Stryx librarian admitted. "I guess the form title is his idea of a joke."

"We adapted the form to the database fields used by the Eemas dating service to get a discount on the station librarian's back office services," Chastity admitted to her reporters. "Besides, there's nothing wrong with getting the basic information like height and eye color on the record."

"Would the candidate rather eat dinner in a fancy restaurant or enjoy a cozy meal at home?" Bob read out loud from his tab.

"It appears that rather than incorporating your hard work, Jeeves simply replaced every instance of 'Would you,' with 'Would the candidate,' in our standard questionnaire," Libby said apologetically. "I just sent an updated version reflecting the changes you actually asked for, and it will be available by the time I finish speaking."

# Fourteen

"I'm not real sure about this," Joe admitted to Woojin, as a crowd of aliens began forming a line in front of the folding table the two men had just carried out to the training area in Mac's Bones. "Given our partnership with Drazen Intelligence, I can see hiring some of their under-employed actors to make our training more realistic, but it looks like every alien on the station showed up for the casting call."

"It's above my pay grade," Woojin replied complacently. "From what I heard, when Clive brought the idea up with Herl at the President's reception, the Horten military attaché just happened to be standing where he could listen in. Ten minutes later, Ambassador Ortha met with the president and demanded to know why the Horten reenactors weren't invited to the auditions."

"I don't understand why Horten reenactors are so keen on working for EarthCent Intelligence. Last thing I knew, they all looked down on humans as being Stryx pets."

"According to Bork, some of the Hortens are hard up for enough hours to keep their union cards active. Besides, alien attitudes towards humans have been shifting rapidly in the last few years. I think they're finally getting used to us."

"That explains why the Horten Stage Actors Guild is demanding that I register Mac's Bones as an official performance venue, but who invited all of these other aliens? If I didn't know better, I'd say that the nervous-looking fellow in the yellow beret there is the Vergallian undercover agent who Beowulf sniffed out on our first day of training camp."

"You should ask him."

"Beowulf? It happened before he was reincarnated and I don't know if those memories carried over."

"I meant the Vergallian."

"It's a thought. But doesn't Clive realize that some of these aliens will be equipped with in-eye recorders so that all of the agents they come in contact with will immediately be blown for undercover work?"

"When did we start sending agents to alien worlds on undercover missions?" Woojin asked, shooting his friend a skeptical look. "Besides, Clive initially plans to try the alien trainers on the newspaper correspondents who actually have a more immediate need. He and Blythe both take the long view, so they want to see EarthCent Intelligence build the internal expertise for our own people to play the part of aliens for training purposes at some point in the future. We've been relying on holograms and Shuk outings for all of our alien environment training, and since the recruits know that they're dealing with 3-D images and market vendors, it's not that realistic."

"I just wonder if we can trust some of these aliens," Joe reiterated. "Imagine a reporter on a Dollnick world asking for directions to a press conference if a Dolly actor intentionally taught him all the wrong words."

"Our own implants will know the difference," Woojin pointed out. "What we're looking for isn't that different from what a commercial traveler might get out of a one week immersive language and culture course. And it's just an experiment at this phase."

"You and I picked up enough Vergallian to get by in a slum, but I never could have become fluent. I used to think that human hearing wasn't capable of registering the fine tonal variations that can change the meanings of the words completely around, but Samuel seems to have a gift for it."

"I try Vergallian on him from time to time and he never misses a beat," Woojin said. "He must practice with his Stryx friend, Banger, because it seems to me he started speaking like a native at some point after Alia left."

"She was a sweet kid." Joe glanced sadly at the ceiling of Mac's Bones, as if he were replaying her departure in his head. Then he set his empty coffee mug on the folding table and checked the time on his heads-up display. "We're open for business in two minutes, but I still wish I knew how the auditions expanded beyond Drazens and Hortens."

"I'll bet the alien performance artists have their own subculture, just like mercenaries," Woojin said. "We never had much competition for cannon fodder jobs, but when it came to a punitive expedition against a rich pirate strong-hold or off-network actions with a chance for prize money, all of a sudden every alien mercenary in the sector would be there to sign the rolls."

"True enough. Here comes Thomas, so we may as well get started."

"Great turnout," the artificial person said, approaching the pair of ex-mercenaries behind the table. "Where's Lynx?"

"Security detail for the president and first mistress," Woojin replied. "She's not even armed, but some alien cultures won't take a leader seriously unless he has some staff in tow."

"Has Chance turned up yet?" Thomas continued.

"I haven't seen her," Joe said. "Have you tried a ping?"

"Do you ping Kelly when she's running late?"

"I have Libby do it for me," Joe admitted. "Kelly's not as sensitive about reminders from the Stryx."

"Here she comes now, Thomas, with the ambassador, Samuel and Beowulf in tow," Woojin said. "Chance must have stopped in to invite them." Beowulf and Samuel veered off to inspect the line of aliens, while Chance and Kelly joined the men at the table.

"This reminds me of the Carnival try-outs," Kelly observed, "except they aren't throwing things and they're much better behaved. Who got them to form a line like that?"

"They did it themselves," Joe replied. "I guess it's not a first casting call for any of them."

"I'm ready to get started," Chance said. "I worked up a few basic scripts in all the standard languages to see how well they interact with me in realistic encounters."

"What exactly are you looking for?" Kelly asked.

"Some alien acting traditions are intentionally artificial," Chance replied, raising her voice so that the applicants could hear her. "For example, Verlock actors would never consider working without their traditional masks made from compressed volcanic ash, and Farlings only give vocal performances from behind a screen. We're looking for trainers who can work naturalistically with a human partner using simple training scripts. It's not dramatic work."

A number of disappointed Verlocks and a giant beetle stepped out of the queue, but over fifty aliens remained.

Chance gave the culled species a minute to say goodbye to the acquaintances whom they only met at open casting calls, and then she turned to the first actor in line.

"Language?"

"Vergallian."

Chance called up the appropriate script and handed her tab to the actor. Joe nodded to Woojin and both men flipped the mental switch to turn off their translation implants. Joe assumed that Chance was fluent in a number of alien languages thanks to her secret agent upgrade from QuickU, but it would be interesting to see how well the artificial person actually spoke it. The boy and the dog returned from inspecting the aliens just in time for the first audition.

Chance put on an ingratiating smile and spoke her part in Vergallian from memory. "I'm here on assignment for the Galactic Free Press to cover the ballroom dancing championships."

"Do you have press credentials?" the Vergallian read from the tab.

"I'm Chance. My name is on the list."

"I can't find your name here," the Vergallian responded, looking rather blank. "Is it possible you put the pass in your change purse and got it mixed in with your creds?"

"Thank you," Chance said. "Give your details to Thomas and we'll be in touch. Next?"

The Vergallian's shoulders slumped at the brisk dismissal, but it was all in a day's work for an unemployed actor.

"Why did she stop him?" Samuel asked his father. "He speaks almost as well as a real Vergallian."

"What?" Joe said, turning towards his son. "He's not Vergallian?"

"I think he's human," the boy said. "I guess he could be some other species, but definitely not Vergallian. Couldn't you tell?"

"Why are you trying to pass as Vergallian?" Joe demanded of the disappointed actor in English.

"I haven't had a good audition since I arrived on Union Station and I'm getting desperate," the man admitted. "Nobody is hiring human actors, and I grew up in Vergallian space so I thought I'd give it a shot."

"Why don't you apply to EarthCent Intelligence for an analyst job?" Thomas asked him. "We can always use people who understand alien languages without implants."

"I'm an actor," the man said indignantly, straightening himself up. Then his shoulders sagged again. "How's the pay?"

While Thomas explained the employment conditions of EarthCent Intelligence, Chance selected the script for the next actor in line, a towering Dollnick.

"What are you doing here, little human?" the Dollnick demanded. Joe heard the line as a series of whistles and bird calls and realized he hadn't turned his translation implant back on.

"I was looking for the prince's summer pavilion, but I seem to have gotten lost," Chance trilled and tweeted back.

"You'll never find your way without help," the Dollnick asserted, working himself up into a rage. "How much money do you have?"

"Excellent," Chance said, retrieving the tab. "Give your details to Thomas and I'm sure we'll be in touch. Next?"

A pale yellow Horten stepped forward and presented the artificial person with an aluminum wafer the approximate size of a business card.

"What's this?" Chance asked.

"My chit," the Horten explained. "You have to register that I showed up for the audition or I could lose my actively-seeking-work allowance from the Guild."

"Don't you want to wait to find out if you got the job first?" Kelly asked.

"I never get the job," the Horten replied dolefully. "They always say I look too nervous."

"We're fine with your color," Chance told him. "Most Hortens turn a little yellow when talking to humans in any case."

"Really?" The Horten immediately turned pink with joy and pocketed his chit. "Where's my script?"

Chance punched up the Horten script and handed over her tab. "You have the first line."

The Horten's lips moved silently as he read through the script to himself. He turned yellow with white spots as he got into character and his expression became dour. Finally, he placed the tab on the table and confronted Chance aggressively.

"Stop right there," he said. "No dogs or Humans allowed."

Beowulf let out a rumbling growl and rose to his feet, his shoulders coming up to the same level as Samuel's.

"Okay, we'll take the dog, but not the Humans," the actor ad-libbed.

"But we have a reservation on this shuttle for Horten Eight," Chance replied in fluent Horten. "Our team is here to cover the gaming tourney."

"What do Humans know about gaming," the Horten replied scornfully. "Run on home to your Stryx and get the news off the Grenouthian network!"

"That was perfect," Chance said, picking up the tab. "Give your information to Thomas and we really will be in contact. Next."

A young Drazen male leaned on the table and leered at Chance. "Hey, baby. Looking good. If the gig involves playing with you, I'll take it

"First we have to see if you're up to the challenge," Chance responded with a saucy grin. She pulled up the appropriate script on her tab. "I've met plenty of Drazens who talked like big men, but when push came to shove, they could barely read a menu."

"That's because we eat everything," the alien retorted, but after taking the tab, his face fell. "Why'd you write the script in High Drazen?"

"You don't speak High Drazen?"

"Of course I can speak it, but I haven't ever seen the need to learn the musical notation in order to read it. It's only used by news commentators, diplomats, people like that. When I've played aristocrats in daytime immersives, the High Drazen is always transliterated for the scripts."

"I can read it," the female Drazen behind him spoke up. "We all do. The boys don't pay attention in school."

"We were really looking for actors capable of playing a wide range of roles, including diplomats and officials," Chance said to the young male.

"I told you I can speak it fine. Hey, how about writing it out for me phonetically," he continued, turning his charms on the Drazen female.

"Do you have a quota for the number of Drazens you're hiring?" the female asked Chance.

"Yes, but we definitely want to split it between males and females," the artificial person replied.

"Alright. Let me go first and see if you can remember the lines," the female told the male. He handed her the tab and moved grudgingly aside.

"Ready?" Chance asked. Receiving a nod, she continued with her lines from memory, "Is this drink safe for humans?"

"Will you be taking it internally or externally?" the female read.

"Neither."

The Drazen woman erupted in musical laughter and turned away for a moment to regain her composure. "I'm sorry, can I go again? The idea of a human wanting to buy a Divverflip is just too funny."

"I know exactly what you mean," Chance said, winking at Thomas. The two artificial people still had difficulty understanding why humans went to such lengths distilling alcoholic beverages that they couldn't enjoy without watering down. "Is this drink safe for humans?" she started over again.

"Will you be taking it internally or externally?"

"Neither. I was hoping it would dissolve the scale in my coffee maker," Chance replied.

"I'm sure if you boil a couple pots of water afterwards it will be fine," the Drazen woman asserted, before going off script again "Is that a poison sensor ring you're wearing? It's very tasteful."

"I like yours too. If you add your contact info to my tab, I'll ping you later with the job details."

"Can I go now?" the Drazen male interrupted. "If you chicks keep chatting, I'm going to forget my lines."

Chance accepted her tab back from the female and turned to the male. "Is this drink safe for humans?"

162

"Will you be taking it internally or externally?" the Drazen male asked.

"Thank you," Chance said in Drazen. "Give your contact information to Thomas and we'll be in touch. Next?"

The Drazen opened his mouth again to protest, then thought better of exposing himself to further humiliation and moved sulkily away. Chance extended her tab to an open space in front of the table, where it seemed to levitate.

"How did you do that?" Samuel asked.

"Please turn off your invisibility projector so the boy can see you," Chance told the floating tab. A cheerful Chert materialized in front of the table. "Are you sure you'll be comfortable interacting with people while visible?"

"I'm fine with it," the humanoid replied. "But I heard that you were looking for actors to help your secret agents cope with stressful situations involving other species. If I was training Humans to keep their heads around Cherts, I'd want them to practice talking to empty space."

"That's a good point," Thomas interjected. "But then, what do we need to pay you for?"

"Oh," the Chert replied, and vanished.

Chance retrieved her floating tab and called, "Next."

"I hope you don't discriminate against AI," said a large cylinder on wheels.

"No, of course not," Chance reassured the bulky robot. "I have a script for AI right here."

A pincer extended from a slot in the robot's casing to take the tab, and Beowulf gave a sharp bark.

"That's his Jeeves bark," Samuel cried.

"Jeeves?" Kelly asked. "Are you in there?"

A ghostly pair of eyes appeared on the cylinder and shot the dog a disgusted look. Then the metallic shell split apart revealing Jeeves. The Stryx rapidly crumpled the metal halves of the cylinder into a small ball using manipulator fields, and then tossed it to the other side of the training grounds. Beowulf took off in pursuit.

"Is he going to hurt his teeth on that?" Joe asked.

"I do it all with holographic projections, he's more likely to bite his tongue," the mischievous Stryx replied. "I can use the same technique to impersonate any AI you can imagine. I'm sure your hiring practices don't discriminate against artificial intelligence."

"Actually, I'll be disappointed if we can't find any alien AI to work with," Chance said, extending her tab to Jeeves. "Shall we do the first encounter scenario?"

"Right," Jeeves replied, floating a little higher and giving himself a half-spin to settle into his role. Then he proclaimed in an artificial voice, "Prepare to die, biological scum."

"But I'm from Earth and we're a Stryx protectorate," the artificial person protested. "I'm also friends with the great and powerful Jeeves, and if you—hey, stop sticking lines in my memory, you Stryx creep! Give me back my tab. You just failed the audition. Next."

"Go easy, Chance," Thomas protested. "He's just having a bit of fun. I'll bet he'll work really cheap."

"That's right," Jeeves declared, reluctantly handing back the tab. "And I'm not a union member so you can abuse me."

"I'll bring it up with Blythe and Clive," Chance said, though her tone made it clear that she intended to forget. "Now move aside and let the aliens who really need the work have their chance. Next?"

# Fifteen

Affie came to an abrupt halt and regarded Dorothy with pity, as if the girl had admitted she could neither read nor write. "You've never been in a fitting room?"

"I've tried things on in a boutique," Dorothy replied defensively. "They have sizes based on your height, weight and measurements, but it doesn't make much sense."

"Tried things on?" the Vergallian asked incredulously. "As in, you take off your own clothes and then put on something that a hundred other people have worn?"

"Not a hundred, I don't think. And it's kind of fun since I only go with my Mom or with Chance. She's got great taste."

"So whoever you go with tells you if the dress fits?"

"Well, they have mirrors, too."

"Mirrors?" Affie shook her head. "I knew you guys were a bit slow on the technical front but I didn't think it was that bad."

"Well, how does everybody else do it, then? Why hasn't it even come up in my Open University design courses?"

"Did you count on your fingers when you were a little girl?"

"Of course. Well, my friend Metoo said it wasn't fair since he didn't really have fingers, so I learned to count in my head," Dorothy explained.

165

"And do you see anybody counting on their fingers in the Open University?"

"Do you mean that all the other species know about fitting rooms from childhood?"

"Exactly," Affie said, steering Dorothy into a side alley of the upscale retail section on one of the Vergallian decks. There she stopped and took a last critical look at the human girl's face. "If it wasn't for the red hair, you could almost pass, you know. A little shadowing would bring out your cheekbones and hide some minor asymmetries."

"Pass as Vergallian?"

"For a couple years, maybe, until your skin begins to age," Affie said matter-of-factly. "I asked the station librarian about your biology and it was a little shocking."

"How old are you, Affie?" Dorothy asked, suddenly curious.

"In your years, forty-two," the girl replied.

"That's more than twice as old as me!"

"You have to look at it in relative terms. You're old enough to get married, but I won't be able to have children for at least another ten years or so. We just age and mature at different rates." The Vergallian girl looked around as if she was searching for something. "I would have sworn there was an avatar parlor around here somewhere."

"I thought we were going to a fashion outlet to try things on."

"That was before you said you've never been to a fitting room. We need to get your avatar first."

"What's that?"

"Another you, for the fitting," Affie said in exasperation at her friend's thick-headedness. "There it is, let's go." She led Dorothy into a narrow shop lined with doors. The waiting customers were all Vergallians, some mothers with children, but mainly adolescents.

"This is embarrassing," Dorothy muttered. "They're all kids."

"It's just that you have to come in a lot more often when you're growing," Affie explained. "I haven't needed a new avatar in years. Look, the self-service one is open."

"But I don't know what I'm doing," Dorothy protested.

"It's easy, the attendants are really just there to help with complicated clothes, the kind your maid helps you remove." She lowered her voice. "Not that the customers here can afford servants, but it's a cheap way to pretend."

"I have to take my clothes off?"

"Unless you're shopping for dresses to wear over what you have on now, it would be a good idea." Affie opened the self-service door, deposited a one-cred coin in the slot, and pushed Dorothy in. "Just strip down and do what the voice tells you to do. It only takes a couple of minutes."

"Everything?" Dorothy squeaked, as Affie began closing the door.

"Don't be a baby. You can keep your undergarments on if you don't expect to do any lingerie shopping," she added, seeing Dorothy's obvious discomfort. "I'll guard the door."

The room was long and narrow, with a series of rails running along the walls and ceiling. There was a small bench to her left and a number of hooks with clothes hangers on the back of the door.

"Please remove your clothes," a voice intoned in Vergallian. "Three minutes to avatar construction."

"Libby?" Dorothy subvoced. "Is it safe in here?"

"I have no records of any accidents taking place in an avatar parlor," the station librarian replied.

"I mean, will my pictures be kept private?"

"No images will be created. The parlor uses low-power lasers to take your active measurements for creation of an avatar. It's just a large set of numbers and vectors and you retain sole ownership."

"But couldn't they be used to create holographic images?"

"As long as you only use your avatar crystal in certified fitting rooms, the transferred data is restricted to temporary memory. Fitting rooms are a big business for Horten manufacturers and they take the security very seriously."

"Two minutes to avatar construction," the room announced.

"Thanks for reminding me," Dorothy said sarcastically, but she stripped rapidly to her underwear, thankful she was wearing sandals and not laced boots.

"Please walk towards the green light," the voice said, just seconds after she finished disrobing.

"This better not hurt," Dorothy grumbled, walking down the track. A veritable battery of moving lasers painted her from head to toe at every possible angle, reminding her of a scene from an old movie of a ground vehicle on Earth going through an automated car wash. When she reached the end of the short runway, the voice began issuing a series of rapid-fire commands.

"Touch the red lights to your sides, now reach for the blue lights above your head. Sequence fail. Touch the red lights to your sides, now reach for the blue lights above your head. Second sequence fail. The Vergallian Clothiers Guild requires that you be notified that three sequence failures in a row results in avatar construction termination without a refund. Touch the red lights to your sides, now reach for the blue lights above your head. Thank you. Walk towards the green light above the entry door. Thank you. Place your right foot on the bench. Exchange your right foot for your left foot. Sequence fail."

"But I didn't understand the instruction," Dorothy protested.

"Place your right foot on the bench," the voice continued. This time, Dorothy didn't hesitate in taking her right foot down and putting her left foot up. "Touch your toes. Stand up straight. Lunge to your left. Lunge to your right. Crouch. Spin to your right. Your other right. Spin to your left. Jump. Higher. This construction session is completed. You have three minutes to dress. Thank you for your business."

Dorothy hurriedly pulled her clothes back on and was slipping into her sandals just as the buzzer sounded. She opened the door and stepped out of the avatar booth, feeling a sudden chill.

"You're all red," Affie exclaimed, looking concerned. "Do you have a skin allergy to lasers? I'm so sorry I dragged you here."

"I'm just embarrassed," Dorothy admitted, feeling somehow better that she had given Affie a shock. "I've never paraded around in my underwear for a disembodied voice before. Was all that bending and stretching really necessary?"

"You want your clothes to fit while you're moving, don't you?"

There was a clattering sound like a pebble tumbling down a rainspout, and a small, transparent cube rattled into the catch basin under the coin slot. Dorothy retrieved the avatar crystal and squinted at it, as if to make sure there wasn't a visible image of her trapped inside.

"What do I do with it now?" the ambassador's daughter asked her Vergallian friend.

"Now we shop," Affie declared, linking arms with Dorothy and leading her back out into the corridor. "This whole section is women's clothing stores, including accessories and shoes. But now that you have an avatar, you'll want to see a real dress in a shop with a fitting room."

"Nothing too expensive," Dorothy reminded her.

"How much can you spend?"

"Maybe fifty creds?" the girl replied tentatively. She arrived at this figure by adding the emergency twenty-cred coin her mother insisted she keep as a reserve to the current cash value of the programmable cred piece through which the Stryx paid her for working at the lost-and-found. Affie guided her through a one-hundred-and-eighty-degree turn and then headed in the opposite direction, away from the main corridor.

"I know a place that gets the latest fashions from the Empire but at Dollnick knock-off prices. You can never be sure when they're open though, because they get raided from time to time."

A harried-looking Vergallian male approached the friends as they entered his shop and he addressed Affie politely. "Are you shopping for yourself or your servant?"

"Both, and she's my friend, not my servant," Affie replied, using the inflection on the Vergallian word for 'friend' that indicated a relatively new relationship with a fellow student who was perceived as a social equal.

The shop owner hid his surprise and spoke directly to Dorothy. "Are you looking for something in particular today?"

"Affie said that you carry the latest Empire styles, and I was hoping there might be something that suits me,"

Dorothy replied. "I'm also doing field research for my work in fashion design at the Open University."

"Do you mean a sort of an investigation?" the man asked nervously. He backed up a few steps and pulled a small device that looked like some sort of controller from his pocket.

"Just relax," Affie said. "My friend isn't an undercover agent for the fashion police. She just got her first avatar," the Vergallian girl continued, trying to put the shop keeper at ease. "Humans usually try things on until they find something that fits."

"This is a prank, right?" the man said, peering out the front of the shop to see if an immersive crew from one of the candid camera shows was lurking. "It's really her first avatar?" The girls nodded solemnly. "Then I shall have the honor of selling the young, ah, sentient, the first dress she's ever owned that fits."

"Is there an open fitting room?" Affie prompted him.

"Certainly," the man replied. "Do you wish to browse the floor inventory before entering or will you choose from the catalog."

"I think we'll go with the catalog today," Affie said.

The salesman led the girls to a blank sheet of black, wall-height glass, and made a lifting gesture. The glass shot up into the ceiling, and the girls entered a small room with a Vergallian-style sofa against one wall and an articulated metal arm with a device resembling a mini-register sticking up from the floor. After Dorothy and Affie took their seats, the man made another gesture, bringing a holographic catalog into existence.

"Items with a blue star aren't currently in stock but can be imported within a quarter-cycle. Just slot your crystals into the receptacle and you can get started." He remained

171

long enough to see Affie slot her crystal into the device on the floor-mount. The black glass wall reappeared as soon as the man stepped out of the fitting room.

"Just put in your crystal and say your name," Affie encouraged Dorothy. "It's just so the fitting room can tell who's who."

"Uh, Dorothy," the human girl said, putting her new crystal into the device. "What now?"

"Pick something you like from the catalog," Affie said. "Touch the image and say your name, or advance to the next collection with a gesture, like this." She swiped at the curved hologram like she was spinning a prayer wheel, and a new set of dresses on unbelievably perfect Vergallian models rotated into view.

"It's intimidating," Dorothy complained. "They're all so beautiful."

"They're professionals. A lot of daughters from the high-caste families do modeling before they get married. I tried it for a couple cycles, but it was exhausting, and the old duchess who owned the agency kept hinting that I should lose some weight."

"That's crazy. You're like a size zero already."

"How can anybody be a size zero? That makes no sense."

"I looked it up a couple years ago. After they established a system on Earth where the smaller numbers were supposed to be better, they changed the scale every decade so that the skinniest women could claim a smaller and smaller size. After zero, they went to double-zero, and then they started multiplying by the square-root of negative one and calling them 'imaginary sizes.' The whole thing got so ridiculous they had to go back to zero as the ultimate."

"Now you're pranking me, aren't you?" Affie asked with a skeptical look.

"Do you want me to ping Libby for the proof?"

"Never mind. We're here to shop, even if it's homework for you. Just pick something to see how it works."

Dorothy leaned forward and poked an elegant evening gown, saying her name as she touched it. The catalog disappeared, and a perfect hologram of herself materialized out of thin air and twirled. She watched in shock as she saw herself reach above her head, touch her toes, and then amble gracelessly around the room.

"You walked better than that when you were high on Kraaken stick," Affie observed. "You're hunched up like you expect something is about to attack you."

"I was embarrassed," Dorothy said. "I didn't know. Libby? Can you fix my avatar?"

"That will be two creds," the station librarian replied.

"You're going to charge me?"

"It's written into the lease for the avatar parlors that we won't undercut them by providing freebies for station residents," Libby said apologetically. "I have to charge double their rate by contract."

"It's worth it," Affie told Dorothy. "Just have her take it out of your pay."

"Alright," Dorothy grumbled. "Don't tell my mom about this, either of you. She'll say I should have gone back to the avatar parlor and done it again."

The holographic projection of Dorothy wearing the dress winked out, and then came back, looking even more life-like than the real girl. Dorothy watched in awe as the more elegant version of herself strolled across the room in high heels, a designer purse sparkling with fake diamonds clutched in her hand.

"I borrowed the vectors for some of Chance's shoes and bags with her permission," Libby reported. "The selection will appear along the top of the store catalog when you bring it back up."

"Two creds was a bargain!" Affie enthused. "My avatar was done by a specialty outfit for the modeling agency, but it can't adjust for the heel height so seamlessly."

"What do you think about the dress?" Dorothy asked, half-hypnotized by a vision of herself she had never imagined could exist.

"Price," Affie said out loud, and some Vergallian script appeared floating along above the hologram's head. "Ooh, two-twenty. I guess that's out of your range unless you want me to loan it to you."

"No, no," the girl protested. "I can't imagine when I would ever get a chance to put it on. David would run the other direction if he saw me wearing something like that. I look like an immersive star or something." She blushed at her own words. "You try a dress now."

The Vergallian girl waved Dorothy's hologram out of existence and called up the catalog again. After selecting a V-shaped dress with pointy shoulders that stuck up to the eye-level of the catalog model, she asked, "Could I borrow a pair of Chance's shoes?"

"It's okay by me," Dorothy replied. "Does it work that way, Libby?"

"Let me check with Chance," the station librarian replied. "She says it's fine, but if you break a heel you have to replace them."

The two girls looked at each other in puzzlement.

"That was an artificial intelligence joke," Libby added.

"Oh, I get it," Dorothy said, and gave a polite laugh.

"Let me have the adjustable waltz shoes with the figure eight heel," Affie instructed the station librarian. "Can you set the height to seventy percent?"

A hologram of a very haughty Affie strutted towards the girls, looking exactly like a model on a catwalk. Stopping right in front of them, the avatar struck a number of odd poses that accentuated lines of the elegant dress.

"Wow, that dress fits you like a second skin," Dorothy told her friend.

"I look like a Trelling with those shoulders," Affie replied dismissively. "And if I ever got Stick out on the dance floor and he dipped me, I could put somebody's eye out with those points." She waved the hologram out of existence and the catalog returned. "Your turn."

"This is so cool," Dorothy said, picking a plain frock that she thought might not be too expensive. "With the low heels, please, Libby. And don't bother with the bag."

Dorothy's avatar reappeared, skipped across the room, and turned a cartwheel in front of the startled girls. Then a hologram of David popped up across from her, dressed in his usual jeans and T-shirt, and the two figures went into a sort of two-step, the only dancing style the young man seemed to understand.

"I've never seen a dance partner in a fitting room before," Affie exclaimed. "Why don't they all do this, Librarian? Is this a Stryx patent that they can't afford to license?"

"I'm afraid it would be difficult to achieve with commercial technology," Libby said apologetically. "I'm kind of cheating and reallocating resources from other tasks. If I charged the same rates I do for computational commercial work, this presentation would cost approximately eight creds a second."

"Shut it off!" Dorothy croaked. "I can do the two-step with David for real and all it takes is some pleading."

# Sixteen

After popping two recently reattached buttons off of his best shirt, Joe muttered something about shrinkage and slipped past his wife and out of the bedroom.

"Get back here," Kelly called after him. "Your uniforms aren't shrinking, you're expanding, and another beer is only going to make it worse."

Joe ignored his marching orders and continued down to his brew room, where he retrieved an elastic metal back brace from the wall. It was traditionally worn by Frunge males during their ancestor worship ceremonies, a ritual nearly identical to the Scottish sport of caber toss. Czeros had given the belt to Joe as a present after an evening of manly commiseration about lower-back problems.

The owner of Mac's Bones had just switched from half-kegs to quarter-kegs in his microbrewery due to his body's complaints about liquid weight-lifting. The Frunge worship belt helped a great deal, and it had the added benefit of acting as a male girdle. He lifted up his T-shirt, sucked in his gut, and wrapped the alien support around his midsection. The two ends of the belt seemed to merge into a single elastic metal band when he pressed them together, creating an invisible seam. He pulled down his T-shirt and headed back upstairs.

"I put the buttons back on with Horten thread glue so we don't lose them, but I guess you're going to have to find something else martial to wear," Kelly said. "What are you doing?"

"It'll be fine," Joe asserted, taking back the shirt and easily making the buttons. "I just did a few sit-ups to tighten the old abdominals."

"Baloney," Kelly muttered, but she was too busy preparing herself to investigate the mystery of the vanishing beer belly. "Are you going to carry any weapons?"

"I'll borrow Ian's old Claymore, the one he hangs over the bar, and Wooj said he's bringing a Vergallian saber. Nobody would expect Clive to carry visible arms since he's a spymaster, and Lynx is scary when she glares."

"And the four of you will be enough?"

"Four would be overkill as an honor guard for anybody except the Dollnicks, and with them it's just a symmetry thing," Joe replied. "All of the aliens know it's purely ceremonial in any case, but they'd think less of the president if we didn't make the effort. Who are the princes the Dollnick ambassador is introducing?"

"Drume, from Chianga, and Kuerda, from one of the big terraforming clans. Chianga is one of the open worlds with a large human presence, and Kuerda's family has the contract to terraform Venus."

"I hope the president has something more to offer them than Sheezle larvae," Joe said, pulling a black baseball cap over his short hair. "Why is the meeting at Pub Haggis rather than some fancy restaurant on a Dollnick deck?"

"The president knows that nothing on the station is going to impress a Dollnick prince, so he's falling back on his grandfather's philosophy for approaching bankers."

"Which was?"

"His grandfather ran a machine shop back before the Stryx opened Earth, and whenever he got a big order, he'd

177

need a bank loan to cover materials until he could deliver and get paid. Stephen's mother told him that they always knew when his grandfather was going to the bank because he'd get up in the morning and put on his work clothes from the previous day. He wanted the bankers to think that he was so busy that he had to work around the clock."

"The president is going to wear dirty clothes to the meeting?"

"Hildy wouldn't let him, she's got more sense than that. But the idea is that Pub Haggis is more workman-like. Plus, it's not a secure location."

"That's a plus?"

"The Dollnick ambassador and the princes will no doubt have their personal scramblers that prevent eaves-dropping, but the president wants to make sure that word gets out he's meeting with them. It should help push forward the negotiations with other aliens."

"Pretty smart," Joe admitted.

"The president wasn't very happy when his private conversation with Hildy was blasted all over the Grenouthian network, but he was quick to see how we can use them to our advantage. If we leaked a story to the Galactic Free Press about the meeting, everybody would take it with a grain of salt, but when the bunnies report the story, it will gain instant credibility."

"You asked to be alerted fifteen minutes before your appointment," Libby's voice came from nowhere and everywhere. "I pinged Hildy as well, and they're waiting for you in the living room. Clive, Woojin and Lynx are on their way to the Little Apple."

"Thanks, Libby," Kelly replied. "We're leaving now."

Ten minutes later, while Joe retrieved Ian's sword from behind the bar, the president went over last minute strategy notes with Clive and Blythe, who had been sounding out alien contacts on possible joint ventures for Earth.

"Do you think there's really a chance they'll be willing to train terraforming engineers on Earth?" the president asked. "I can twist the arms of some old national governments and throw in a desert or two as practice areas if the Dollnicks are serious about it."

"We have a better chance of getting them to set up some assembly plants with an apprenticeship program, the way they do it on their own worlds," Blythe said. "Just learning how to work with alien equipment is a good start, and I'm sure you've seen the floaters the humans on Chianga are producing based on Dollnick components and modified designs."

"The Dollnicks are the biggest employers of human labor, with over a billion of us working on their ag worlds or terraforming projects," Clive added. "They've even repurposed some of their heavy equipment for two-armed operators. If you can just get them to invest in a few Earth factories, vocational and specialist training will surely follow."

"But a university extension campus is out of the question?" President Beyer asked.

"They don't really have universities on their own worlds, just colleges for the liberal arts. Technical and scientific training is all provided on-the-job in apprenticeship programs."

"Alright. Anything else I need to know?"

"Keep the good side of your profile to the falafel stand," Blythe told him. "Here they come. Everybody look professional."

The president rose to meet the Dollnicks, and Kelly, Hildy and Blythe gathered around him. The ceremonial bodyguards, Clive, Woojin, Lynx and Joe, formed on either side of the human delegation, trying their best not to look silly.

"Ambassador Crute," Kelly said, inclining her head. "The President of EarthCent extends his thanks for your arrangement of this meeting."

"Of course," the alien diplomat replied brusquely. "Prince Drume and Prince Kuerda need no introduction in civilized space, so let's begin."

The Dollnicks seated themselves on the extra-high chairs that Ian had rented for their use, and their own bodyguards moved to strategic locations around the room. Donna had reserved the whole restaurant for the event, and other than the conspicuous group of aliens with immersive cameras gathered at the nearby falafel stand, the meeting was completely private.

"I understand how valuable your time is so I'll get right to the point," the president began. "The EarthCent administration is opening Earth to direct alien investment. We've already closed a deal with the Verlocks to establish an academy for theoretical mathematics and magic, but we're particularly interested in putting our population on a sounder technological basis."

"You wish us to train humans to compete in our markets?" Prince Drume asked, folding all four of his arms across his chest.

"Not to compete, to contribute," the president said enthusiastically. "You're already the biggest employer of human expatriates, and surely there must be times when you wish that our people came to you with a more practical skill set. Establishing pilot manufacturing or assembly facilities on Earth would give you the chance to screen for employees worthy of recruitment for service in your many admirable businesses."

"While there is truth in your words, we anticipated your proposal and our projection for the return on capital isn't worth the effort," Prince Kuerda stated bluntly. "A local staging base to assemble equipment for the next phase of the Venus terraforming project would be convenient, but paying cancellation fees to the orbital factories already contracted to do the work would offset any gains."

"But you came to the meeting," the president observed.

"I recently received an interesting report from the director of our mining firm, which employs Humans in asteroid scouting," Kuerda continued, looking directly at the president. "There was a mention of certain stores of thorium existing on Earth, though the report was somewhat confused about the provenance. Perhaps it was hoarded as treasure by your pre-Stryx governments?"

"Thorium?" The president glanced to his left at Kelly and Hildy, who shook their heads, and then turned to Blythe, who poked his shoulder and leaned over to whisper in his ear.

"Nuclear waste," she murmured. "Spent fuel from power reactors and fissile materials from weapons programs. We used to trade it in the virtual game world, but there didn't seem to be any point in looking into it as a business because of the radioactivity. It's dangerous for humans to transport and the old governments had all sorts of regulations about it. Try them on uranium and plutonium."

"Ah. That thorium," the president said to Kuerda. "Yes, along with uranium and plutonium, I believe we have quite a bit saved up around the world."

All three Dollnicks gaped. "Quite a bit?" Kuerda croaked. "And you don't keep it all in one place under lock and key to prevent theft?"

Blythe broke off her hasty subvoced conversation with the Stryx librarian and whispered in the president's ear again.

"It's not all high-grade," the president hastened to add. "Some of it is in the form of mine tailings, and I'm told that the, er, half-life of certain isotopes is unfortunately all too brief. But I'm sure a species with your technical ability..."

"You can sell the mine tailings to the Drazens, they like that sort of thing. I must insist on exclusivity for all of your high-level radioactive reserves to maximize our return on the reprocessing and packaging facility. We will pay ninety percent of the Frunge spot price minus the cost of shipping to an appropriate market in return for building the reprocessing plants and training human operators."

"That sounds quite fair," the president said, glancing left and right for input from his brain trust. According to the EarthCent Intelligence assessment, Dollnick princes would only be offended by any attempt to negotiate an offer, the details of which would then be sorted out by underlings.

"Deal," Kuerda said. The giant Dollnick displayed his knowledge of human etiquette by extending all four of his arms across the table to shake hands with the president and the three women simultaneously. Then he turned his head to one of his bodyguards and called, "Get a Thark recorder in here." The Dolly nodded and whispered into a device on a wristband.

"That's fine for you, Kuerda, but I'm not looking to expand my commodities business," Prince Drume observed. "I'm here because I've been favorably impressed with how

182

the Human contract laborers we've brought to Chianga have established successful enterprises after completing their terms. They're surprisingly diligent about keeping up with their loan payments."

"There are still more than four billion people on Earth and no shortage of willing borrowers," the president said. "The problem is that our higher education system is primarily focused on self-replication."

The Dollnicks nodded, and Prince Drume said, "It's an occupational hazard in all non-vocational education systems. That's why our own industries utilize on-the-job professional training. I suggest you do the same."

"That's an excellent idea," the president replied, as if he were hearing it for the first time. "If only we had the industrial infrastructure in place to train a new generation of engineers, but unfortunately, our world was just completing the transition to a service economy when the Stryx arrived."

"You mean everybody worked for your military service? My intelligence shows no evidence of a modern weapons industry on your world."

"Our nations had to give up on weapons development when most of the people left to become contract laborers for generous alien employers such as yourselves. The governments basically remade themselves into pension funds for their retired workers," the president explained. "The service economy that evolved on Earth was based on people providing advice for each other, things like that. It was much more lucrative than manufacturing products."

"But where did the money come from?" Drume asked. "How was value created?"

"You don't remember the Grenouthian documentary?" Kuerda said to Drume, with a significant look at his fellow prince. "They printed the money on slips of special paper or they added to the supply electronically with primitive computers. It's what led the Stryx to step in and open Earth, since they'd never seen sentients so bent upon self-destruction by economic means."

"That was a documentary? I thought it was the pilot for a new post-apocalyptic series," Drume replied in astonishment. He turned back to the EarthCent president. "Perhaps you'd like to hire us to govern your world?"

"We're getting better at it now," President Beyer declared hastily. "But if you could see your way to taking over a few of our abandoned industrial parks and setting up some manufacturing facilities, I can grant you extraterritorial status. That will give you immunity from taxes, regulations, and interference from anybody claiming to have authority over the area. You'll have to operate within Stryx rules, of course, since we remain a protectorate."

"Perhaps some of my own Humans will be interested in managing such a project for me," Drume mused. "I seem to recall that Earth lacks vehicular levitation technology, so a floater assembly plant such as the one on Chianga would be a possibility."

"That would be ideal," the president replied. "The old roads on our world are so broken up that wheeled vehicles are next to useless outside of the major routes. Once people start buying floaters, they'll be even less willing to pay for road maintenance, and you'll end up owning the whole transportation market."

"You will guarantee us a monopoly in any advanced manufacturing process we bring to Earth, of course," Drume asserted.

"Of course," the president replied. "Our underlings can negotiate the exact time limit for the monopoly, but I have no problem with it extending beyond my own lifetime."

"Deal," Drume said abruptly, and reached across the table as Kuerda had done to shake hands with the humans. As soon as he leaned back, Ambassador Crute whispered in the prince's ear, who look startled and exclaimed out loud, "That short?" He turned back to the president of EarthCent and asked, "How old are you now?"

"Fifty-one," Stephen replied.

Drume grimaced and let out something untranslatable that sounded a little like 'tomatoes' with a fingernails-on-a-chalkboard screech mixed in, causing all of the humans to cringe.

"That's fifty-one across!" Kelly exclaimed, her eyes lighting up. "Dover. It's been driving me nuts all day." Then she remembered where she was and tried to look suitably embarrassed, but she couldn't stop grinning with satisfaction all the same.

"I thought you promised to stop working the cross-words on your heads-up display," Blythe reminded her.

"I did stop, but one or two tricky clues still get imprinted on my brain, and the answers come to me at the oddest times," Kelly said.

"It's a form of addiction pushed by our local news business to build a subscriber base," the president explained to the Dollnicks. "Some people compulsively check spot prices for commodities, others try to figure out what word fits in a numbered space based on vague clues."

"The crossword puzzles aren't a hide-in-plain-sight communications method?" the Dollnick ambassador asked. "Our intelligence people have been wasting valuable time trying to solve them, and I understand that several

185

junior analysts assigned to the task have required medical attention."

"But they publish the solution the next week," Blythe pointed out.

"We assumed that was a disinformation ploy," the ambassador admitted. "Do I have your word that you aren't using this method to communicate with undercover agents in Dollnick space?"

"We don't have any undercover agents in your space," Blythe protested. The three Dollnicks regarded her skeptically. "Ambassador McAllister. While we're waiting for the Thark recorder, why don't you explain the word you just solved so the Dollnicks will understand that it's just a puzzle."

"Alright," Kelly agreed readily. "The title of this week's puzzle was 'Alien Substitution,' which is an obvious hint that sometimes the answers relate to aliens or are just stand-ins for the word that fits. When the president gave his age, I couldn't help thinking about that clue in the puzzle. I was sure about the 'v' in the middle of fifty-one across and the 'r' at the end, but the clue was _ _ _ _ _hanger, which means the first five letters of the word were missing. At first I thought the fifth letter would be a 'c' which would make the rest of the clue into 'changer' or…"

"Don't chase the Dollnicks off before we get the contracts recorded," the president whispered.

"Oh, so when Prince Drume, uh, reacted to the president's age, it reminded me of chalkboard scraping, and that's when it hit me."

"When what hit you?" Hildy asked.

"Cliffhanger. Isn't it obvious?"

"How do you get from 'cliffhanger' to 'Dover?'" the president demanded.

"You know, the white cliffs of Dover. It's a substitution. And they're white because they're chalk, which squeaks on blackboards, though it's not as bad as fingernails," she concluded happily.

"I think you can instruct your cultural attaché to stop wasting time trying to break the Human puzzle encryption," Prince Kuerda advised Ambassador Crute openly. "Even if they are sending secret messages, it's unlikely their agents can understand them."

"I hate substitutions," President Beyer muttered darkly.

The Thark recorder arrived, looking a little like royalty in his ceremonial robes, and took a seat at the table without being asked.

"Have you recorded a contract with us before?" the Thark addressed the humans.

"Yes," Kelly and Blythe replied together, but the president shook his head.

"Very well," the Thark said. "The process is quite simple. You will establish your identities, speak the terms of your agreement, and I will record them." The recorder touched a pendant that hung around his neck and said, "Party one consists of Princes Kuerda and Drume, whose identities are known to all, and Dollnick Ambassador Crute as witness. Party two consists of…"

"President Stephen Beyer of EarthCent, negotiating for Earth," the president said.

"Ambassador Kelly McAllister as witness," Kelly added.

"I positively identify Ambassador McAllister from the Carnival race," the Thark continued. "Can somebody vouch for the EarthCent president?"

"I can," Kelly said.

"I meant somebody with financial standing," the Thark told her bluntly.

"Blythe Oxford. I can vouch for him. I've recorded dozens of Thark contracts."

The recorder turned his attention to Blythe, and nodded in the affirmative after using an overlay image on his heads-up display to confirm her identity. "If any of you are acting under duress, this is the time to say something," the Thark declared formally. "Very well. Should I assume that this will be a standard Princely contract of intent, with the details to be negotiated at a later date?"

"Yes," the Dollnick princes and the president replied together.

A few minutes later, after the contracts guaranteeing the Dollnicks monopolies on reprocessing and exporting Earth's nuclear waste and establishing privileged factories were spoken, the Thark stated, "Recorded."

# Seventeen

"So you're on an alien planet and your external voice box fails. What do you do?" Thomas challenged the young reporter, identified as 'Thad' by the badge hanging around his neck.

"Find another one?"

"There isn't another one. Members of most planet-based species go through their lives without encountering aliens unless it's on vacation, so they don't need translation devices."

"But how do they communicate with members of their own species who speak a different language?"

"All of the advanced species have long since standardized on a single language, though in many cases there's a more formal or expanded version used by a particular segment of society. Even if planet-based aliens have implants, they aren't going to waste space storing human languages on the off chance you might show up on their doorstep to report a story."

"But we could still understand them, right?" asked a young woman with a pageboy cut.

"Yes, but asking questions is an important part of the job for newspaper reporters," Thomas pointed out.

The second one-week kidnapping avoidance class was populated by recent Galactic Free Press hires with little or no experience, and Joe had warned the artificial person that it would be very different than training experienced correspondents. Thomas had hoped to move quickly through the basics, but he hadn't expected all of the trainees to be youngsters who had just aged out of a labor contract or recently arrived from Earth. A dozen Drazen and Horten actors had clocked-in and were waiting in the practice area to engage the humans in loosely scripted scenarios.

"Do we use sign language?" another youngster asked.

"Give us an example," Chance urged her, strolling up to the group.

"Well, I could point at my mouth if I was hungry," the trainee replied.

"Or maybe at your belly," another said.

"I'd make cutting up food and eating motions," Thad contributed, complete with a pantomime demonstration.

"So depending on the species, they might think you are threatening to eat them, indicating that you're carrying a child, or playing an imaginary stringed instrument that required you to keep wetting the bow with your tongue."

"She's exaggerating," Thomas reassured the youngsters, some of whom were looking around like they were think-ing of bolting. "There's a much simpler fallback solution when you're dealing with biologicals whose vocal speech falls in the range that humans can reproduce."

"Are you saying we have to start learning alien lan-guages?" the first young man asked hesitantly. "I grew up on a Dollnick ag world, and I can whistle at most a dozen words that a Dolly who didn't know me might actually understand."

"Dollnick is a particularly difficult language and much of it takes place at higher frequencies than humans can hear," Thomas replied. "You'll find that the more human a species looks, the more likely you can replicate their speech to some degree. Common Vergallian and Horten are easily transliterated into English, most of the Chert language can be managed if you stay away from numbers, and you can get by in Drazen if you talk to the males. The Drazen females speak a super-set of the language based on musical notes that humans would need a synthesizer to reproduce. It's also possible for motivated humans to learn enough Verlock to communicate, but most of those who do so lose their facility to speak human languages at the normal pace."

"If I have to learn an alien language well enough to ask questions, I may as well leave now," said the young woman with the pageboy cut.

"Now who's scaring the newbies?" Chance declared, shoving Thomas aside. "You all have in-eye recorders with heads-up display capability or you wouldn't be here today. What we're going to start with this morning is the transliteration mode your implant provides. It's a fall-back for emergencies, like if your voice box batteries run down, or if it gets stepped on by a large amphibian."

"I just got my subvoc pickup and I haven't learned how to use it yet," a young man said. "How will the translation implant even know what I want to say?"

"The transliteration mode can also work like an external voice box set to voice control. You'll say what you want out loud in English, and a phonetic representation will appear on your heads-up display. But it won't do much good unless you get into the habit of practicing with it. Today you'll get the chance to try it out with native speakers, but in the future you can take advantage of the delay and practice by yourself."

"How does that work?" Thad asked.

"A delay? The implant simply waits the delay interval you specify before translating, so you can speak a phrase in English, read the transliteration out loud, and then you'll hear the implant translate what you said. In fact, you should all set your implants to transliteration and delay mode right now. All set? Good. The temporary venue contract we signed with the Horten Stage Actors Guild kicks into 'Golden Time' in three hours and eighteen minutes. After that we have to pay triple the rate, which of course means the Drazens will want the same or we'll have a war on our hands, so hold on to the rest of your questions until after lunch and let's get started. Thomas?"

"If each of you will look at the back of your name badge, you'll see a number which will correspond with the number on the badge of one of the alien trainers. In the first exercise, you'll approach the alien assigned to you and ask for directions to the nearest spaceport. Understand?"

A chorus of uncertain-sounding responses greeted the question, but the young reporter trainees allowed the two artificial people to herd them over to the practice area, where the aliens were awaiting them while drinking from a variety of take-out beverage containers. The nearest Drazen wore the numeral "one" around his neck, which happened to match the number on the back of Thad's name tag. The young man approached the Drazen cautiously.

"Excuse me, sir. Could you tell me the direction to the spaceport?" There was a short pause, and then the would-be reporter began sounding out phonetic transliteration on his heads-up display. "Hrrt Shigabit. D'she, uh, mechkrwynk gchuchh..." Thad broke off after beginning to choke on his own gutturals. Luckily, the spasm of coughing caused his head to duck just in time to evade a roundhouse punch thrown by the enraged Drazen, whose tentacle was sticking up like a flagpole behind his head.

"Hey, no hitting," Thomas shouted in Drazen, leaping towards the pair and catching the alien's six-fingered fist before he could reload for a second try. "What's the problem?"

"He said I don't have a sense of humor," the angry Drazen shouted, struggling against the artificial person's vise-like grip. "Nobody tells me I don't have a sense of humor."

"Thad? What did you say to him?"

"I just read what was on my heads-up display," the young man protested. "Wait, I'm getting the delayed translation now." Thad turned pale and backed away from the Drazen. "I guess I said he doesn't have a sense of humor and he's never known trouble, but I didn't mean to."

"Drazens, Hortens, huddle up," Thomas shouted in both alien languages, motioning the aliens to gather around him. "Change of plan. Turn your implants back on so you can understand what our people are saying and then correct their pronunciation as required."

"So we're working as voice coaches now?" a Horten actor asked slyly.

"No," Chance interjected before Thomas could reply. "According to Subsection 724, paragraph 71 of the temporary agreement under which you are employed, you are all working at the impersonator pay scale, even if your roles require you to venture into other areas."

"Who am I supposed to be impersonating?" the Horten demanded.

"A Horten voice coach," Chance replied sweetly. "I was in the room when our management went over all of this with your union rep, so don't try to renegotiate a contract that's already been signed. Who's the steward here?"

A short Horten with blue-tinted skin reluctantly set aside the drink he'd been sucking at through a squiggly transparent straw and addressed the malcontent. "Leave it, Thunta. We're getting paid scale and the Humans agreed to fractional pension points, even though we aren't working a full Grether. If you want to go home, I have fifty-seven actors on the bench waiting for a chance."

Thunta turned yellow, streaked with red and grey, but clamped his jaw shut and backed down.

"Did everybody see that?" Thomas asked the trainees. "When you're talking to Hortens, the color of their skin is as important as what they say. While there's no universal guide, you can assume that angry Hortens will turn some shade of red and happy Hortens will appear brown. Now find your counterpart and let's start over."

"I'm sorry about what I said earlier," Thad told his Drazen trainer under the watchful eyes of Thomas. Then he repeated it from the transliteration, managing not to choke this time.

Even though the Drazen now had his implant turned on and understood what the young man was trying to say, his tentacle stiffened at the human's botched pronunciation.

"First of all, you're saying 'hoo' when you mean to say 'kchoo,'" the Drazen informed Thad. "Just say 'kch' for me."

"Chi," the young man said hopefully. The Drazen shook his head and sighed. Thomas patted the alien on the back, carefully avoiding his tentacle, and moved on to the next human-Drazen pair.

As the morning wore on, it became clear that the trainees were much better at pronouncing Horten than Drazen.

194

All of them mastered the idiosyncrasies of the English-to-Horten transliterations for speaking simple phrases, and one of the girls who had a knack for it was already able to sustain a sort of conversation.

"So, how did you end up here?" Gail asked her partner in stilted Horten sounded out from the transliteration.

"I heard through the grapevine that the Stryx were hiring actors, but it turned out they only wanted war reenactors for some sort of theme park attraction."

"And you can't afford a ticket home?"

"You just asked if I couldn't afford a mud-brick home," the Horten corrected her. "You have an excellent ear, but I suspect you are running up against the limitations of the simple transliteration system you described. I believe you have the aptitude to master the Horten character set, which I strongly suggest."

Gail blushed at the compliment from the alien. "You mean, I could learn how to pronounce the letter combinations in your language without knowing what they mean?"

"I'm sorry if I've made you angry," the Horten apologized, his skin tone shifting from dark brown to something shading towards yellow. "Did I say something wrong?"

"What? Oh, I get it. You're asking because I turned red. I'm just not used to compliments. Normally men only say something nice to me if they want—never mind. Do you really think I could learn to read Horten script? I've seen it in corridor ads and it looks pretty difficult."

"It can't be any more difficult than the bizarre system your own people use. And learning to sound out the words without understanding them is actually quite common among Hortens, since worship of Gortunda is performed in the Old Tongue, which uses the same alphabet."

Chance nodded in approval at the Horten trainer's explanation and made a note on her tab before moving on to the next pair. As soon as she was out of earshot, the Horten who had brought up the coaching pay issue leaned over and whispered angrily to Gail's trainer, "Slow up. You're going to kill the job. If she nails it down today, they won't call you back tomorrow and then maybe she'll put ME out of work."

"What did he say?" Gail asked her partner.

"That if I play my part too well I'm going to put us out of work prematurely," the Horten replied. "There's one like him on every job, but I don't bite the hand that feeds me. Besides, I'm here on a one-week trial engagement, and unlike that Grubnick, I actually studied the scripts. I'm looking forward to moving past emergency language training and on to the encounter scenarios. They leave us plenty of room for improvisation, which is my specialty."

Twenty steps away, Thad had pretty much given up on pronouncing Drazen words without permanently damaging his vocal chords, and was instead peppering his trainer with cultural questions in English.

"What's it mean when you scratch your head with your tentacle like that?"

The Drazen actor absently scratched his head with his tentacle before replying, "I have an itch?"

Next to them, a young woman accidently coughed up a ball of phlegm while trying to say the Drazen word for 'pleasant', which could only be pronounced from the back of the throat. Thomas leaned in and caught the projectile with a handkerchief that he whisked out of the breast pocket of his suit. He looked at the silk handkerchief sadly and called the group to attention.

"Fine effort, people. Trainers also. We'll swap groups tomorrow and try it again so our trainees can see if they have an aptitude for sounding out the other language. For now we're going to move on to the loosely scripted scenarios, and if you can't make yourself understood with the transliteration, just speak English and let the implants do the work for both sides. Pull up your scripts and let's see how you do."

The Drazen working with Thad had memorized the script and launched into his role immediately. He took a step back and raised both of his hands to his face, turning them flat so it looked like he was creating a shelf for his chin.

"What are you doing?" Thad asked, not sure if this was part of the scenario. The other trainees and actors turned to watch.

"This is a restricted area, Human," the Drazen snarled, at the same time making little head nods towards his hands, which Thad now gathered must be an alien analog to holding out an arm with the palm raised. "State your business."

"I'm a foreign correspondent for the Galactic Free Press," Thad replied in English, one of the suggested responses from his own script. "I'm here to report on the launching of your new colony ship."

"The colony ship dry dock is on the other side of the orbital," the Drazen snapped in response. "This is a closed military facility."

Here the script on Thad's heads-up display presented options rather than instructions. Giving up sounded like an attempt to winnow out spineless reporters, and trying to dash by the guard seemed a bit extreme, so he chose the middle path of attempting to persuade the Drazen to let him in.

"I'm sure they're expecting me," Thad ad-libbed, putting on a friendly smile. "The newspaper I work for is practically an arm of EarthCent Intelligence, and I hear they have a close relationship with Drazen Intelligence."

The actor playing the guard narrowed his eyes and reached behind his back for an imaginary weapon slung over his shoulder. Gripping the shaft of what was now clear was supposed to be an axe with both hands, the Drazen asked Thad, "Did you just say you're a spy?"

The reporter trainee took a step backwards, holding his hands out in what he hoped would be seen as a placating gesture as he stared at the invisible axe head. "I think there's been a mistake," he said hastily. "You know how inaccurate translation implants are. I'll just head over to the other side of the orbital where I'm supposed to be."

"Halt!" the Drazen commanded. "I'm contacting my superior officer for instructions."

Caught up in the scenario, Thad turned and began to sprint in the opposite direction, leading the Drazen to reach way back and execute a two-handed overhead throw of his imaginary double-bladed battle axe.

"Dead," Chance proclaimed, stopping Thad in his tracks. The Drazen actors all burst into cheers and congratulated their fellow on his accurate throw. "Could you tell the rest of us why you chose to run from a suspicious alien guard rather than walking away from a polite rejection?"

"I thought you wanted me to show initiative," Thad said. "I was worried I might fail the training if I didn't get the story."

"That was last week when you were learning about reporting from the editorial staff," Chance scolded him. "This is the week we try to teach you not to get kidnapped or axed in the back while running away from a guard."

"I think that was instructive," Thomas told the group. "Would anybody else like to demonstrate their technique before you all begin practicing?"

"We'll try it," Gail called, volunteering herself and her Horten trainer.

The actors and trainees formed a loose arc on either side of the pair, like living parentheses, and the Horten launched into his part.

"Welcome to planetary decontamination control. Place your clothing in the deposit chute and step into the shower booth."

"I'm afraid there's been some mistake," Gail replied in her sounded-out Horten. "I went through decontamination on your orbiting platform and was given a clean bill of health before I took your shuttle service to the surface."

"There are space rules and ground rules, and I make the ground rules," the Horten replied firmly, not bothering to lift his eyes from the imaginary passenger manifest he held.

"I understand what you are saying and I appeal to your empathy as a fellow sentient," Gail said, choosing the 'humble negotiation' option from her script. "Disrobing in front of others is uncomfortable for many members of my species and I'm afraid I'll turn bright red if I try."

The Horten looked up, and his own skin began shifting from a neutral beige to take on a golden hue. "It does seem unfortunate that you must go through decontamination twice in one day, but like all civilized species, we fund our customs and immigration services with fees. Since you aren't importing anything…"

"I see," Gail replied instantly. "How much would you charge for a thorough decontamination from a visitor who required the procedure?"

"Shall we say, a hundred Stryx creds?" the Horten suggested, the golden hue of his skin becoming more pronounced.

"As a working reporter, all of my expenses are paid through a programmable cred coin," Gail responded, watching the Horten closely. His hopeful expression became surly and the golden hue began to dull.

"We've had problems with programmable creds creating unnecessary audit trails," the Horten said, looking back down at his tab. "Place your clothes in the chute and step into the shower."

"I do have some cash," Gail hastened to say. "Just not a hundred creds."

"How much?" the Horten asked bluntly.

"Maybe twenty?" she ventured.

"Maybe forty?" the Horten counter-offered.

"Maybe thirty, so I'll have ten left for emergencies," Gail pleaded, guessing that his imaginary tab might include imaging capability that was seeing into her imaginary change purse. The Horten immediately turned a cheery brown.

"Please deposit your foreign currency in the chute for decontamination," he said with a broad grin. Gail opened her imaginary purse, counted out some imaginary coins, and dropped them in the chute. "Your decontamination procedure is complete," the actor continued. "Welcome to Horten Four. Enjoy your stay."

The gathered humans and aliens all burst into applause at the performance, causing Gail to blush again, leading the Hortens to point at her in amusement.

"How did you do that?" she asked her trainer afterwards. "I thought adult Hortens couldn't control their skin colors."

"I'm a professional actor," the Horten explained. "When I submerge myself in a role, my skin response is just reflecting what I'm feeling. You really seem to be a natural at this yourself. I shouldn't wonder if with sufficient practice we couldn't teach you to turn some new colors."

# Eighteen

"You know, it's not really considered proper for a girl my age to go into business with, uh, aliens." Flazint nervously twirled a stray hair vine onto one of her fingers and then let it go. The vine retained its spiral shape as if it had been trained on a trellis. "You're saying that we three will be the design department and that you have some other people lined up to handle all of the business issues?"

"Two humans and a Stryx," Dorothy confirmed. "If you watched the Kasilian auction like ten years ago, you saw them all on stage at the same time running the show. Shaina and Brinda are sisters who grew up selling stuff in the open-market, and Jeeves is, well, Jeeves."

"He's the Stryx robot who came and took you home after you passed out from inhaling Kraken stick," Affie said. "I wasn't sure how long you'd sleep since you're Human and all, so I pinged the station librarian for help. Before Stick and I even finished our drinks, Jeeves showed up and carried you off in a manipulator field. He was pretty cool for an AI."

"Jeeves brought me home?" Dorothy cringed in embarrassment. "I didn't remember anything after the Drazen bar exhibit, but I guess I assumed you put me in a lift tube and I made it home by myself. I hope my parents didn't see me."

"You shouldn't inhale that stuff, especially if we're going to be in business together," Flazint admonished her.

"Once was enough for me," Dorothy promised. "So what do you say, Affie? Can you spare the time from your studies, or are you in a big hurry to finish these?" The human girl swept her arm around the Vergallian's sculpture studio where they were meeting to discuss the new business. The room was filled with pieces of various sizes crafted from different materials, and all of the works resembled blobs connected by cubes.

"These are all finished already," Affie replied with a smile. She was tickled to find that her new friend was familiar with abstract art humor. "What do you really think of them?"

"They're inter—uh—interrogative," Dorothy said desperately. The two other girls waited expectantly for her to explain. "I mean, like, they ask a question about the galaxy, you know, uh, or at least, that's how I see them. How about you, Flazint?"

"The colors are nice," the Frunge girl replied. Affie looked pleased by this assessment, and the human girl filed it away in her memory as an acceptable reaction to alien art.

"So, are you onboard with the cross-species fashions idea?" Dorothy prompted Affie, anxious to move on from art criticism.

"Sure," the Vergallian girl replied. "I came here to be on the cutting edge and Humans are the current disrupters. So is the idea to stick with hats for now, or are we going to start working our way down towards shoes?"

"Shoes are way too complicated for a near-term goal. We'll have to work our way up to them," Dorothy corrected the Vergallian.

"But hats are at the top and shoes are at the bottom on all of the humanoids I've seen," Flazint objected. "Feet are down by definition."

"I'll bet it's another translation thing," Affie guessed. She'd already learned that limitations of the Human dialect Dorothy spoke prevented the nuances of High Vergallian from carrying over, but this was the first time she'd noticed a problem with such a simple phrase. "I just assumed that all sentients had an expression that corresponded with 'working your way down,' to get to something more important. You know, like, working your way down to be boss."

"It's 'working your way up,' with us," Dorothy told them.

"Weird," Affie said. "So if you want to find out what's really going on, do you say, like, I'm going to get to the top of this?"

"The bottom of this," Dorothy admitted.

"At least we're all agreed that the important stuff is at the bottom," Affie said, and Flazint nodded her agreement.

"Oh, alright, I don't want to get hung up on semantics. I just meant that we should move beyond hats, but let's save thinking about shoes for when we have more experience."

"As long as I get to work with metal," Flazint interjected. "I don't care if it's just buckles and clasps or the occasional mesh, but I want to apply something from my education. Besides, if my family thought I was going over to fibers they would disown me."

"You see, that's exactly why I said that designing cross-culture requires a multi-species team," Dorothy continued. "If we're going to come up with a line of clothing and accessories we can sell to all of the humanoids, we have to go beyond aesthetics and look at the whole sentient."

"The Horten hat trick you pulled off by sorting through the last six thousand years of their fashions in the lost-and-found was genius, but will it apply cross-species?" Flazint asked.

"If it was just the hats, I would have dumped the whole business off on Jeeves and company for a royalty. But when Chance and I returned to the lost-and-found to look for other examples of evolving fashions, she got discouraged because we kept coming up with look-alike products that were actually from unrelated species at different time periods."

"So you gave up on the idea and now you want to design things from scratch," Affie concluded.

"Just the opposite. I realized that humanoid fashions repeat across all the bi-pedal species, just not at the same times. I was talking about it with Aisha since her parents are in the specialty clothing business back on Earth, and she pointed out something I'd missed entirely since I don't watch her show anymore."

"They do a really cool feature once a cycle on the mystery of children's clothing," Flazint interrupted. "I couldn't believe some of the memory metal items the Verlocks make for their kids. They even have a type of mitten that if you lose one, you can manipulate the survivor into a hat or a pair of thin socks." The Frunge girl caught herself sounding uncool and mumbled, "It's not that I'd watch it myself, but my little brother is afraid to be alone when there are Grenouthians in the hologram."

"I didn't even know that Aisha was doing clothes," Dorothy admitted. "What she told me is that the feel of the show has completely changed since she started. It turns out that the alien children she recruits these days have watched LMF for at least a year before they join the cast. So they already know that all the other little aliens aren't going to eat them and that they can all be friends."

"And you think that her show is starting a galactic trend in tolerance?" Affie asked.

"Maybe the show is part of a trend rather than the root cause, but there's clearly something going on," Dorothy insisted. "I checked with Libby, and interspecies tourism is up like a thousand percent over the last decade. She says there's always an uptick when they bring a new species onto the tunnel network, but that's a thousand percent on top of the boost from when the Stryx opened Earth, and it's accelerating. Don't forget you're the one who told me that humans are like cat lists before I, like, fell asleep and Jeeves took me home."

"Catalysts," the Vergallian informed her, and Flazint burst out laughing so hard that her hair vines were in danger of losing a few leaves.

"You were high on Kraken stick and it made sense to you that Humans are like cat lists?" the Frunge girl asked when she caught her breath.

"Well, there are all kinds of cats and people bring them on colony ships to catch mice," Dorothy defended herself. "I thought Affie meant that even though we're not as advanced as some species, we come in all shapes and colors and we contribute when you least expect it."

"No, I really meant catalysts," Affie said seriously, sending the Frunge metallurgy student off into fresh gales of laughter. "It's like you make certain reactions possible just by being there and providing some missing element. Flazint could explain the importance of catalysts if she could stop laughing. I bet someday a Verlock xenosociologist will come up with a mathematical proof of what I'm saying, not that anybody other than the Verlocks and the Stryx will understand it."

"But my cross-species fashion idea isn't an attempt to start a movement or anything," Dorothy protested. "It's just a way to break into the business so that later we'll be able to get our original designs into production. I have lots of good ideas for jumpsuits."

"So we all understand each other then," Flazint said, finally regaining control over herself. "You've already transferred your book of hat orders to the management team, right? How come you didn't invite Chance to our meeting?"

"I did, but she wasn't interested. She says that clothes are for wearing and she already has one job more than she wants. I did ask Jeeves if he'd be available to talk with you both. Can I ping him and tell him we're ready?"

"Sure," Affie said, and Flazint nodded.

Dorothy barely finished subvocing the invitation when the studio door slid open and Jeeves rolled in.

"Are you grounded for something, Jeeves?" Dorothy asked. She still felt guilty about getting her friend Metoo banned from floating for two days after he fixed the Carnival election for the EarthCent ambassador at Dorothy's request.

"I knew that young Affie is a sculptor and I thought she might be uncomfortable with a bulky metal object such as myself floating around amongst her works," Jeeves replied. "The pieces are interesting. You should invite Dring to see them some time."

The Vergallian girl practically burst with pride at the compliment from the Stryx, and Dorothy kicked herself for changing her own initial reaction.

"I do seem to have a talent for going into business with lovely young females," Jeeves continued, causing Flazint's hair vines to brighten with the Frunge equivalent of chlorophyll. "Let's just get the contractual stuff out of the way and then I'm anxious to listen to your ideas."

"What sort of contractual stuff?" Dorothy asked.

"Your employment agreement with SBJ," Jeeves said casually. He projected a hologram of a dense document in an unknown language, which reminded Dorothy of the cuneiform tablets from a Grenouthian documentary on Earth's history. "It's just the standard boilerplate for being in business with a Stryx partner and I'm sure you're all familiar with the terms. Just give your verbal acceptance and I'll file it away."

"I can't even read it," Dorothy complained, turning to her two friends. "Can you?"

"I'm sure it's alright since it's a Stryx contract," Flazint said.

"It's not like he could have any possible reason to cheat us," Affie added.

"Libby?" Dorothy called out loud.

"Yes, Dorothy?" the Stryx librarian replied through the magic of the station's infrastructure.

"My mother told me never to agree to a contract on the station without checking with you first, and I can't even read what Jeeves is offering us."

"That's because my offspring chose Akkadian for his composition," Libby replied. "I suppose it was an appropriate selection since there's something in here about taking possession of your first-born child, and, oh dear, he seems to have lifted a whole section from the End User License Agreement for our diplomatic implants. You shouldn't agree to this."

"Never mind," Jeeves sighed, and the holographic contract vanished without a sound. "I was going to use it as a teaching moment for the young ladies, but I guess nobody trusts anybody anymore."

"Why do I get the feeling that working for Stryx Jeeves won't be the same as working for Stryx Libby in the lost-and-found," Flazint said nervously.

"May I clarify a few things before we begin, Stryx Jeeves?" Affie asked.

"Full disclosure is essential to forming lasting business relationships," Jeeves replied.

"Why are you interested in going into business with inexperienced Open University students?"

"An ungrateful artificial person by the name of Chance refused to give me an acting job for which I was exceptionally well qualified, and the auction business is on hiatus so I have some free time."

"I mean, and keep in mind I never met a Stryx before coming to Union Station, but why go into business with biologicals at all? We're not as squeamish in Fleet as some of the planetary-based species, and I know from first level evolutionary biology that somebody has been fiddling with the chain of custody on the genetic mutations that produced intelligent species in this galaxy for the last forty or fifty million years. It's not that I'm complaining, but don't you have better things to do with your time?"

Flazint stuck her fingers in her ears at the mention of evolutionary biology and began muttering "Seedlings, seedlings, seedlings," to herself in an undertone, but Dorothy was fascinated by the direct question. She'd heard rumors that Stryx science ships were responsible for the rise of dog-like creatures on so many worlds, but the idea that the AI may have directly steered the emergence of intelligent humanoid life was new to her.

"Time is not an issue with me," Jeeves answered. "I get pressure from my elders to invest more effort into traditional Stryx studies, but frankly, I've always found math to be a bit of a bore. Surveying the ever-changing multiverse for the sake of making lists is like herding cats."

"But women's clothing and accessories?" Affie demanded. "Why not manufacture spaceships, or invent artificial gravity, or time machines?"

"My elders have established guidelines for sharing technology with less advanced species, and I'm forced to admit that those rules make a great deal of sense. And if anybody ever asks you to invest in artificial gravity or time travel, I advise you to decline. As to my interest in women's clothing, 'Varium et mutabile semper femina.'"

"That's not very complimentary," Dorothy protested, after her implant translated Virgil's saying about the fickleness of women from Latin.

"I'm sure you realize that trade on the tunnel network, like all advanced economies, is driven more by desires than needs." Jeeves responded. "It's the psychology of marketing that I find fascinating, predicting what will be a hit or a flop, discovering the ideal price points for maximum utilization. Some species will stick with a useful product until something quantitatively better comes along, while others change for the sake of change. Women's clothing and accessories are one of the more dynamic portions of any economy so I'll have plenty of opportunities to test my predictive ability."

"When you mentioned pricing for maximum utilization, is that a Stryx term for profit?" Flazint asked cautiously.

"In a manner of speaking," Jeeves hedged. "Economic activity is the lifeblood of the tunnel network, and our goal of maintaining a healthy balance of trade between species while promoting peace and employment opportunities may occasionally require me to invert the profit curve."

"Does that mean you might go to our parents for money?"

"Never," Jeeves said firmly. "I promise that your personal liability will be limited to your investment in sweat equity. But if you'd be more comfortable with a written contract, I had one around here somewhere..."

"Never mind the comedy routine," Dorothy said impatiently. "Can we talk about designing clothes now? I'm really not all that interested in business stuff."

"Very well," Jeeves replied. "Welcome to the SBJ family. I have a large order of hats to see to, so take your time creating our next product and make me proud."

The Stryx floated up off the deck and headed for the door, which slid open at his approach. Dorothy slaved her tab to one of Affie's wall displays, and the three girls began paging through images of the crossover fashions that the human girl had identified in the lost-and-found.

"Pause," Affie told the controller. "That travel cloak reminds me of ones I've seen in period dramas about the Empire. There's a modern version that shows up in boutiques from time to time, but the colors are so garish that only the old women buy them."

"I'd wear something like that but I don't recognize it," Flazint said. "Was it ever a Frunge fashion?"

Dorothy checked her tab. "About four thousand years ago. And they were popular with the upper classes on Earth a couple hundred years ago, both with men and women."

"Any other species?" Affie asked Dorothy.

"The Hortens had a version with a high collar that the women sometimes wore along with a mask to hide their emotions when using public transportation. It covers up their shoulders and necklines, and I wouldn't be surprised if they originally sold them with dresses, as a set."

"So it's a possibility," Flazint said. "Did you find anything we wear in common with the Dollnicks or the Verlocks?"

"Bags," Dorothy replied, tapping at her tab to advance a number of images. "Dollnick fashions go through periods where the females can carry more than one bag, about the only advantage of having four arms as near as I can tell." The Vergallian and Frunge nodded their agreement. "When they only carry one handbag, it's the size of luggage for us, but when they carry two, or even three, some of the bags are the same sizes as ours. The Verlocks have been carrying the same basic bag for hundreds of thousands if not millions of years, both the males and the females, but they go through cycles on the materials."

"Yeah, but they have to be flame-retardant," Flazint pointed out.

"And purses are about the only clothing item Grenouthian females bother with, which is kind of ironic when you consider they have natural pouches," Dorothy continued.

"They dye their fur," Affie commented. "I used to think they were born all those different colors, but it turns out that the females are always changing. We're just lucky to be living in times when they all go for solid colors."

"Do they match their bags to their fur color?" Dorothy asked excitedly.

"I think they do," Flazint said. "I guess that would make them pretty unlikely customers."

"How expensive is the dye they use?" Dorothy followed up. "Could we include it with the purse as a package deal?"

"Maybe we could do that for all the species," Affie suggested. "It's not something I'd go for myself, but some Vergallian women change their hair color all the time."

"I didn't think of that," Dorothy said. "Lots of human women change their hair color too. Maybe we could start a bag-matching trend."

"Don't even think about messing with my hair vines," Flazint warned them.

"But you could match the trellis color if you were doing something fancy," Affie said. "And between clasps and buckles, purses offer plenty of opportunities to get creative with metal."

"Not to mention mesh construction and chain fringes," Dorothy added. "Why don't we all spend some time playing with variations on these historical handbags, and then we can get together and discuss them."

The other two girls agreed, and the design meeting broke up, with Flazint hurrying off for a family meal.

"I didn't want to say anything while Flazint was still here because the Frunge are pretty sensitive about heredity, but did you hear Jeeves admit that they've diddled with the genes of our ancestors?" Dorothy asked.

"Not denying it isn't exactly the same as confirming it," Affie replied.

"But he basically said that they use biologicals as catalysts to keep the multiverse moving along."

"Not in Vergallian, he didn't."

"Jeeves really likes playing with words, and it gives him a way to hint at stuff without getting in trouble with his elders. What else could it have meant when he said that making multiverse lists is like herding cats? He's saying the Stryx are cat listers. Get it? Catalysters. If the word actually existed, it could imply that they work with catalysts. Biologicals."

"You have really interesting friends," Affie replied.

# Nineteen

"How can 'bra' be the beginning of a five-letter word for 'pointers?'" Kelly asked.

"Brass," Joe suggested. "Mercenaries still use it as a slang term for high-ranking officers."

"Oh, that works." Kelly penciled in the letters on the puzzle that Donna had printed for her on an immunization certificate. "Is that because officers point at places to attack?"

"Not unless they want to get picked off by snipers. I'm guessing the puzzle maker was referring to West Point, one of the old military academies."

"You're getting really good at these," Kelly said, looking up from the puzzle.

"It's become self-defense living with you. The other day when Paul pinged me to come and adjust the calliope for the Physics Ride, I asked Sam if he was interested in going for a fly. First he checked that his zipper wasn't undone, and then he asked if I was talking about shopping for fishing lures or swimming in a magnetic levitation suit. It's no wonder he prefers watching immersives in Vergallian these days. At least their language is precise."

"I just need to complete one puzzle without errors and then I'll stop. I'm so close this week that I told Dring not to show me his solution unless I ask for it. There's only one open area left that I can't quite get started on. What's an eight-letter word…"

"I hear Beowulf barking," Joe interrupted, hurrying for the ramp of the ice harvester. "Good luck with the Drazens and the Frunge."

"I didn't hear anything," Kelly shouted after the deserter. She returned to the puzzle and concentrated on coming up with an eleven-letter word beginning with "p" for a dessert topping, the only bridge between a solved section and the final open area. Something about the clue seemed so familiar, as if the puzzle was trying to send her a message. She tried to ignore the insistent beeping sound in the background, making a mental note to ask her mother to stop sending Samuel noisy old games.

"Mom," Samuel called, a few minutes later.

"Mommy is busy right now," Kelly replied distractedly.

"But the oven has been beeping for five minutes. It's driving me nuts."

"Dessert!" Kelly cried, jumping up and running into the kitchen. The Drazen spice cookies that Hildy had made special for their guests were just starting to smoke. She slid the cookies off onto a plate, thankful that Hildy had messed up on the alien measures and made two times as much of the toxic dough as she intended. Along with the previous batch, the Drazens would have a choice between medium-well and burnt.

"Help me with the cheese and fruit platters," Kelly begged her son. "I got distracted with some important work and our guests will be arriving at any minute."

"Where are the president and his mistress?" Samuel inquired, picking up one of the trays.

"Who told you that Hildy is his mistress?" Kelly demanded, following her son to the living area with both plates of cookies. "It's not a nice word."

"Dorothy explained it," the boy replied. "She said it's like a girlfriend, except the man is already married or something. Why is English so weak? In Vergallian, she'd be a 'gillat,' which is the girlfriend of a married man who is no longer with his wife but who can't get divorced for reasons of state."

"What smells like burnt Drazen spice cookies?" the gillat asked as she entered the ice harvester with a large shopping bag. The president came right behind her, loaded with packages.

Kelly abandoned the idea of questioning her son about his odd Vergallian vocabulary and shifted into diplomatic spin mode.

"I baked one batch the way the recipe said, and another batch, uh, harder, since I think that's how Bork likes them. It would have been a shame to just throw away the extra dough. Anyway, I was beginning to worry that you two would be late and I'd have to do all the negotiating by myself."

"After shopping, we stopped by the departure deck and changed our seating assignments for tomorrow," the president said. "It's nice doing something in person for a change. You've probably forgotten what it's like to go through the day without the help of the station librarian, but we don't have that option on Earth." He carried the gift bag of wine from one of the upscale boutiques over to the coffee table and set both bottles on the tray near the cheese platter, which he knew was intended for the Frunge.

"Speaking of Earth, Donna stopped by earlier with a package that just arrived in the diplomatic pouch," Kelly

217

told her live-in guests. "She said you only ordered it last week and you're lucky it got here so quickly."

"Great!" Hildy attacked the box, unpacked a small spray canister, and studied the label for a moment before relaxing. "It checks out, nitrous oxide propellant. I heard that some of the makers use weird chemicals and I didn't want to take any chances. I carry it myself when I ride the subway back home."

"It's some sort of weapon?" Kelly asked. "I can't imagine the Drazens or the Frunge will be impressed by anything that we produce back on Earth."

"They're here, Mom," Dorothy called as she entered the ice harvester. "The two Drazens with Bork look like rich business-types, and the Frunge with Czeros looks like Flazint's great-grandfather."

"Are you staying to meet them?"

"Can't," Dorothy replied. "I only stopped in to drop off my backpack. I've got a meeting with Shaina and Brinda about lining up retailers and then I'm going with David to a thing, so don't wait up."

The tall girl vanished as suddenly as she had appeared. Her mother shook her head and said to the president and Hildy, "When I was her age, all I wanted was to get into a good college."

"When I was her age, all I wanted was to meet girls like her," the president replied, receiving a fist in the ribs from his mistress. "But it's true," he protested.

"And look where it got you," Hildy scolded automatically. The president smiled happily and Kelly shot the public relations expert a questioning look. "Alright, that might not have been the best comeback in this particular case," Hildy admitted.

There were a few friendly barks from the patio area and then the tramp of feet sounded on the ramp of the ice harvester. Both Bork and Czeros had insisted that Kelly not go to any trouble for their meetings with the president, and they assured the EarthCent ambassador that her home-grown hospitality would impress the guests more than a fancy restaurant. Plus, as Bork pointed out, communications security was now better in Mac's Bones than most public places.

"Ambassador Czeros. Ambassador Bork. Thank you for coming," the president addressed the aliens.

"Allow me to introduce two old friends," Bork said, ushering the Drazen male and female accompanying him forward. "This is Winka, who is Director of the Drazen Museum of Science and Technology, and the sorry specimen to my left is Glunk, who failed the diplomatic boards three times before giving up and starting his own business. Winka. Glunk. I present the President of EarthCent, Stephen Beyer, Ambassador Kelly McAllister, and EarthCent's public relations director, Hildy Greuen."

"And this old tree is Vrazel, who manufactures wing sets and other recreational products," Czeros introduced the elderly Frunge.

"I'm not petrified yet," Vrazel growled, pushing his way past the Frunge ambassador and shaking hands stiffly with the president, Hildy and Kelly. "I wanted to personally thank you for helping Czeros with his drinking problem, Ambassador. Our families share deep roots."

"Oh, forgive me," the president said, looking suddenly embarrassed. "I put out a couple of bottles for you gentlemen without thinking."

"Nonsense," Czeros replied, striding over to the coffee table and examining the wine. "An excellent vintage to celebrate the departure of my drinking problem."

"The inspector general is gone?" Kelly guessed.

"Off to bother some other innocent diplomat no doubt. Though the truth be told, she wasn't that bad to be around after she had a few drinks and let her vines down—what she had left of them with that ridiculous buzz cut."

"So let's all have a seat, enjoy a little snack, and then I can start begging," the president suggested cheerfully.

The aliens made themselves comfortable on the over-stuffed furniture, and Hildy transformed herself into the presidential hostess, locating goblets for Czeros and his companion, and donning rubber gloves to expertly mix some Divverflips for the Drazens. Once the cheese, fruit, and un-burnt cookies had been properly dispatched, the aliens sat back with their beverages and waited for the president to make his pitch.

"Earth has its problems," Stephen began. "The number of humans living on alien worlds exceeds the combined number of those who remain on Earth or live independently in space. Our best and brightest ignore the terrestrial university system and look to the advanced species for their role models in science, technology and mathematics."

"I'm familiar with the discontinuities in our own development after encountering more advanced species because it's one of the permanent exhibitions in our main branch," Winka said. "I assume that's why my old friend Bork invited me to Union Station to meet you, and though I doubt that saving artifacts for a future museum of your own transitional period is at the top of your list, I would be happy to consult with your curators."

A look of disappointment flashed across the president's features, but he covered it quickly and continued. "Any help would be greatly appreciated. You might know that the Verlocks have been experimenting with allowing humans to attend a few of their math academies, and this week they agreed to open a pilot campus on Earth. We've signed contracts with the Dollnicks to establish several industrial facilities that will include on-the-job training for human operators, and the Hortens have agreed to a joint venture in game development. Every alien business we're able to bring to Earth represents a chance for humans to learn a new technology hands-on, and to begin building the missing bridge between our knowledge base and what currently passes as low-tech in the galaxy."

"That's exactly why I invited Winka," Bork said, turning to the museum director. "Didn't you tell me that after a half a million years in parking orbit, the Long Shot is in need of a complete overhaul?"

"Yes, but there's no interest from donors in funding the project, and when I tried to get quotes from shipyards, they just laughed at me."

"What's the Long Shot?" Kelly asked.

"The first Drazen jump ship that didn't blow itself up," Winka explained. "You might be surprised to hear this, but when it comes to displays, our museum-goers care more about aesthetics than historical value. As an experimental robot-operated ship with no crew quarters or miniaturization, the Long Shot looks like a crude collection of drive parts. Since our inventory of early jump ships includes several famous and eye-pleasing vessels that opened colonization or contacted alien species, the Long Shot draws very little interest."

"I thought the Humans might be interested in bidding on the overhaul," Bork said, scratching behind an ear with his tentacle. "As long as you deliver the ship to Earth orbit, I'll bet they could work within your budget."

"Is that even possible?" Winka asked doubtfully. "It's difficult enough for our own people to deal with such primitive technology, like shaped magnets and hand-wound coils..." she trailed off and gave Bork a penetrating look. "Would the Stryx allow it? I thought they discouraged transfer of jump technology to backwards, I mean, developing species."

"It's not so much a technology transfer as a job restoring an obsolete museum exhibit, and Humans are already part of the tunnel network," Bork replied. "The problem, as the president so astutely described, is they are unable to bridge the divide between their current technology and the existing state-of-the-art. I thought the Long Shot might help them make the jump."

Czeros groaned out loud at the pun, but Bork looked rather pleased with himself.

"I personally pledge EarthCent's support for the project and I guarantee we'll get it done within your budget, even if I have to sell indulgences," President Beyer stated in a rush. "We're very good with hand-wound coils."

"Well, I'll have to run it by the board but I don't expect any objections." Winka said. She sat back, looking thoughtful. There were a large number of unloved exhibits in the museum's designated parking orbits and dead-storage areas. An inter-species exhibit-swapping program might create excitement for Drazen patrons interested in primitive Earth weapons, as well as benefitting the Humans.

"We Frunge have never been big museum-goers since living with our ancestors provides as large a window onto our past as we can stand," Czeros said. "But as long as we're talking about ancient history, perhaps I can encourage Vrazel to stick a branch in."

The older Frunge glared at his young relation, who simply refilled his glass and took another sip of wine. Vrazel cleared his throat elaborately before speaking. "I employ over twenty thousand workers of all species in my factory on Thuri Minor, but the real estate market is making it impossible to do business on that world."

"I was in the embassy there for a year when I was younger," Kelly said. "I didn't think there was much industry left, other than tourism and vacation home construction."

"Somebody convinced me that building wing sets near the market would result in all sorts of efficiencies," Vrazel replied. "I could be angry, but the land the factory is built on has appreciated more over the last three hundred years than the total manufacturing profits. Funny how life works out sometimes."

"And you're interested in manufacturing wing sets on Earth?" the president asked eagerly. Flying with wing sets had been the must-do activity of resort vacations for over a hundred-thousand years, and the Frunge even made a four-wing variety for the Dollnicks, who looked like giant dragonflies in flight.

"I once visited Earth to see the vast tracts of forest, areas with limited human habitation," Vrazel continued. "An old friend of mine purchased large areas in your Northern Hemisphere with money from selling a problematic world of his to one of your rich entrepreneurs."

"Kibbutz," Kelly confirmed. "My stepson visited there. He said the people who survived were getting along nicely."

223

"Glad to hear that," the old Frunge said. "With the proper guarantees from EarthCent, I am willing to relocate my factory from Thuri Minor to a site on Earth. I may even retire there one day to wander the unspoiled woods. It's very relaxing."

"Our trees aren't sentient, you know," the president said. "I wouldn't want you making a decision based on a false premise."

"Of course I know," Vrazel responded, and barked a short laugh. "That's what makes your forests such a pleasure. On Frunge worlds, any collection of trees that large is bound to include plenty of ancestors who do nothing but complain about how their offspring are neglecting them. Sometimes, it's enough to make me wish we had a paper industry."

Czeros spit his wine all over Vrazel and Kelly. He was so shocked by his distant relative's words that he was struck speechless.

"Oh, don't look so surprised," Vrazel continued. "Why do you think so many Frunge opt for instant petrification or simply disappear in space? I'm looking into alternatives for myself for when the time comes."

"Well, we'd be happy to have you on Earth in any shape or form you'd care to join us," President Beyer said. "And if you decide to set up any joint-ventures with humans, I've been assured that the Stryx will extend their special tunnel rates for shipping."

"And that brings us to my friend Glunk," Bork said. "Tell him about your discovery."

"It's less of a discovery than an observation," Glunk replied modestly. "You know that we Drazens enjoy cross-species cuisine, but we find many of your food exports to be too mild for our advanced palates."

"Indeed," the president replied. "I often had reason to regret our limited digestive abilities in my days as an ambassador."

"Drazens rarely visit Earth due to the strange reaction our tentacles draw from some of your less, shall we say, cosmopolitan citizens. It never occurred to us that so many of you have trouble digesting your own agricultural products that you could be sitting on a potential goldmine without knowing it."

"Such as?" the president said, winking at Hildy.

"On a recent scrap-metal buying trip to a recycling facility called Rojas Two, I was introduced to a product known as 'hot sauce' by the humans working as sorters. They assured me that there are nearly unlimited varieties of peppers on Earth with an astonishing range of potency, and that the black pepper served in shakers at most human restaurants is one of the weakest strains."

"Absolutely true," the president said. "Hildy?"

EarthCent's public relations director retrieved the box that had arrived in the diplomatic pouch and gave each of the Drazens a canister. "It's sold as a defensive weapon on Earth," she explained. "It's especially effective if it contacts the eyes, so please make sure it doesn't splatter."

Bork picked up the plate of burnt cookies, and using a hand to shield against back spatter, sprayed them liberally from the small canister. Kelly immediately began to sweat just looking at the cookies, or maybe a few molecules had escaped from the watered-down stream and found their way to her nose.

"Oh, these are excellent," Bork declared, holding the plate out for his Drazen companions. "And the spray blends so well with the burnt spice taste. I can just imagine the possibilities."

"Don't forget that the peppers are highly diluted in water for the spray," Hildy informed them.

"I'd like to open an industrial-scale food plant on Earth using advanced Drazen processing and packaging techniques," Glunk said. "I believe with the proper marketing, we can make your peppers into a major export category. And I wouldn't be surprised if we can find other neglected agricultural products that can be repurposed for non-Humans."

"It's a weapon and it's a dessert topping," the president joked.

"Pepper spray," Kelly shouted. "That's ninety across. It's a dessert topping for Drazens. I'm going to finish this puzzle before the solution is published tomorrow evening if I have to work at it all night!"

# Twenty

The densely printed banner read, "Congratulations to Vivian and Samuel - First Place Human Couple – Junior Championships." Donna had drawn the line at adding, "Regional Vergallian Ballroom Dancing," since it would have meant shrinking the font so much that the banner would have looked more like warning tape at a crime scene. The fact that the children were the only humans participating in the Vergallian contest had made it much easier to plan decorations ahead of time. The party was held in the dance studio attached to Marcus and Chastity's apartment, where the children trained together three hours a day.

Vivian and Samuel were still dressed in their Vergallian ballroom formalwear, and Donna had confided in Kelly that her granddaughter's gown had cost more than either of them earned from EarthCent in a year. Of course, Blythe could easily afford it, and the nine-year-old girl had looked just as sophisticated as any of the high-caste Vergallian girls at the competition. Samuel wore a rental suit that Dorothy's friend Affie had helped them pick out, a process which included a trip to a fitting room to create an avatar for the boy.

"I still think those Vergallian judges have it in for humans," Joe said to Stanley, who nodded loyally. "I kept my eye on those score cards, and our kids were the only couple who lost points for 'asymmetric lift' and some business about keeping their cheekbones in line. I'm not going to let Samuel get his molars pulled or starve himself before competitions for the sake of more prominent cheekbones, and I'm sure Blythe and Clive feel the same way about Vivian."

"They were just better than us, Dad," Samuel said, embarrassed by his father's blind support. "I'm not strong enough to lift Vivian the way some of those older Vergallian kids can, and some of them have been practicing bone structure alignment with the same partner for ten years."

"Which we can't have done, since I'm only nine," Vivian added. "And it's not Sam's fault about the lifting. I can't jump as high as those Vergallian girls yet, which makes it much easier on their partners."

"If we're going to waste the celebration party assigning blame, then it's my fault for not teaching them better," Marcus said. "The Vergallian techniques I picked up with the Wanderers are all out of date, and if it weren't for those moves that Samuel learned somewhere, they wouldn't have made the finals. I think that placing ninth with just two years practice is a tremendous achievement."

"The students and teacher were equally brilliant," Chastity added in defense of her husband. "And most important of all, your performance actually got the ambassador to stop staring vacantly into the distance and working on crossword puzzles from memory."

"As if I would let anything get in the way of watching my son compete," Kelly retorted. "Besides, I finished that puzzle this morning. I've broken the curse," she added triumphantly.

"You got it all done, no mistakes?" Chastity asked. "I don't think anybody has sent in a solution for last week's puzzle yet, so if you submit it before the new crossword is released tonight, you could win the prize."

"I don't care about prizes, but I wish I knew who created this puzzle so I could thank him," Kelly said. "Usually I get stuck at some point, and then no matter how much more time I spend, I get nowhere. This week's crossword was pure serendipity. Every time I blocked, something would come up in the president's negotiations that got me going again, especially with the borrowings from alien languages and cultures."

"I know I'm going to regret this, but can you give me an example?" Donna asked.

"I needed a five-letter word for 'alien sap' with a 'u' as the second letter, so I pestered poor Czeros about it for an hour since I was sure it must be related to the Frunge. Then we met with the Grenouthians about setting up an immersive technology center on Earth in exchange for a royalty deal none of us quite understood, and it came to me in a flash. Human."

"Huh?" Joe asked.

"Alien sap. Human. The Grenouthians think that we're suckers. Saps."

"That is something to be proud of," Chastity remarked dryly. "I see Walter and Brinda are finally here so maybe he can tell you who created the puzzle."

"Walter!" Kelly cried, waving in his direction. The managing editor and resident cruciverbalist of the Galactic Free Press grimaced at the sight of the station's notorious puzzle-addict flagging him down. Unfortunately, the newspaper counted on the ambassador as their most reliable diplomatic source, so he put on a brave smile and prepared to play dumb about clues.

"We stopped by the office on the way here so I could approve the story about the Vergallian competition," Walter told his publisher. "Got a great picture of the kids for the front page."

"Kelly finished the puzzle this week and she wants to know who created it," Chastity said.

"But it was one of the signed puzzles, last word across on the bottom," Walter replied. "Are you sure you got everything right?"

Kelly's face fell tragically, and she whipped the sheet of paper from her purse. "It can't be," she cried. "All of the down words mesh."

"Let me see that," Walter said, taking the sheet from her. His eyes scanned the puzzle, nodding, and then he made a 'tch, tch, tch,' sound and gave his head a little shake. "Do you want me to tell you?"

"You mean I made a mistake?" Kelly snatched back the sheet and studied the bottom right corner so intently that it was painful to watch. "Don't tell me I messed up on 'effect' versus 'affect'—I've been getting them confused since I was a girl. But it has to be 'effect' or I can't use 'rep' as 'type of government.' I was a little nervous because 'government' wasn't abbreviated as 'gov' but nothing else fit."

"Raj?" Aisha suggested, leaning in over Kelly's shoulder. "You know, the British government in India?"

"But that changes 'constant irritations' from 'peeves' to—'Jeeves?' Oh, no," Kelly went through a series of color changes that would do a Horten proud.

"I can still give you credit if you want to submit the solution," Walter offered kindly. "I was afraid nobody was going to solve this puzzle. I gave up and looked at the solution after a few hours myself."

"Excuse me for a minute," Kelly said grimly, and made her way to the bathroom. As soon as the door was shut, she subvoced Libby.

"Yes, Kelly," the station librarian replied.

"Where's that constant irritant of an offspring of yours?" the ambassador demanded.

"He's left the station for a short business trip. I'm sure he'll be pleased to hear that you solved his puzzle. He created it especially for you."

"I'll bet he did. How did he know what words were going to come up in the Dollnick negotiations or that Joe and Aisha would help me with particular clues. Is he time-traveling?"

"There is no such thing. While it's theoretically possible to find and visit a parallel out-of-sync universe that might provide some guidance, it would be unlikely to reach the level of crossword puzzle clues. Besides, Jeeves hates that sort of math. He's just a very good guesser."

"Or a very good manipulator," Kelly groused.

"A chip off the old AI."

"Was that another artificial intelligence joke?"

"It's not funny if I have to explain it," Libby replied with a sigh.

.............................

Jeeves entered the excursion lock of the Chintoo orbital and rapidly charged and discharged his casing to brush off the dust of interstellar space. The ionized particles practically threw themselves at the polarized filter in the ceiling. He glanced at the secure keypad and casually broke the advanced encryption, allowing him to trigger the inner door to open without going through the tedious business of knocking and identifying himself or bypassing the controls. Then he floated into the clean vacuum of the residential section of the orbital.

"Well, look what the Stryx dragged in," a passing artificial person commented to her companion as he floated by them in the corridor.

Jeeves ignored the pair and rapidly navigated his way through the maze of passages to the section of the orbital where a large number of Sharf-originated AI made their homes. He approached a cabin and knocked on the door with his pincer.

"Come in," the artificial person broadcast in a modified version of Sharf machine language, employing a weaker version of the encryption used to protect physical access to the orbital. Jeeves floated into the cabin as soon as the door panel retracted.

The eyestalks of the occupant swiveled around to study the guest, though the Sharf artificial person remained where he stood, recharging his power cells through the inductive coils built into the walls of a coffin-like cubby.

"Stryx, I see. Are you here to terminate me for some imagined offense against your opaque regulations?" There was no animosity in the message, just a question from a long-lived AI who knew he had cut some corners in his youth.

"No, 34F9ug21," Jeeves replied over the same frequency. "I'm here to price a custom order of hats."

"Then I'm 'Ug' to friends and customers," the artificial person said, slipping out of the charger bay and floating to a workstation on the wall where he enabled a holographic controller. "How much of a hurry are you in?"

"My partners are biologicals," Jeeves replied. "Humans, mainly."

"Ah, so you'll be looking for a rush job," the AI said, paging his way through a holographic schedule. "Pity about their short life spans. Surprising somebody didn't design them better." He turned to Jeeves and dipped his left eyestalk, the Sharf equivalent of a wink. "As it happens, things are slow around here so I can fit you right in. I assume you can provide the tooling-ready plans?"

Jeeves nodded and sent the artificial person the vector-based drawings, calculated down to the last stitch.

"What's with the two empty loops on the front?" Ug asked after rapidly scanning the plans.

"They're for a buckle, no real function beyond aesthetics, though they plan to use some shiny metals to differentiate between consumer quality and a bespoke version."

"And where are the drawings for the buckle?"

"They'll be making them on Union Station, in some cases by hand forging."

"What?" Ug was so surprised that his eyestalks stretched like a cartoon figure going over a cliff. "That will cost your partners a hundred times as much as the hats!"

"More for the gold ones," Jeeves replied, and waved his pincer through a pattern he knew that Ug would register as a shrug. "There's a Frunge metallurgy student involved. You know what young biologicals are like."

"That's why I moved here," Ug said, turning back to the plans. "It's your financial funeral." He paused for a moment, studying the hologram more closely. "I wouldn't say this to just any customer stopping in to place an order, but I don't want to get on the wrong side of the Stryx, so you should know that these hats aren't exactly original. My

233

group made quite a large run of something very similar for Horten pirates a couple thousand years ago, the order ran into the tens of millions of units. But the ribbon was extended with a sort of tail that hung down the back."

"I didn't realize that Chintoo law recognized intellectual property rights. If I ordered knock-offs from you, would that make me a pirate?"

Ug cocked his head at Jeeves, trying to figure out if the Stryx was toying with him. "The hats weren't knock-offs, at least not that I'm aware of. Now that I think about it, using part of the hatband as a tail was the idea of a young Huravian AI interning with my group. The pirates were just regular Horten pirates."

"Now you have me confused," Jeeves transmitted. "What kind of pirates order millions of legitimate hats from a manufacturer?"

"It was part of a big marketing push we made back after retooling from small arms to consumer goods. We got some of our biological Sharf to act as salesmen along the frontier they share with the Hortens. They came up with a catchy slogan about how ordering from Chintoo was cheaper than stealing, and I recall now that we were asked to intentionally distress some of the products with lasers so they looked like pirate booty. Apparently they sold better on the streets that way."

"Learn something new every day," Jeeves mused, wondering what Shaina and Brinda would think of the marketing ploy. "If things are slow, why don't you give it another try?"

"The 'cheaper than stealing' campaign? But we already used it."

"Two thousand years ago," Jeeves reminded him. "Most biologicals have trouble remembering what happened two years ago, or two minutes ago in some cases."

"Why didn't I think of that?" Ug asked, flicking a metallic finger against his own temple in a sign of self-disgust. "Thanks for the tip. The downside of sparing ourselves from biological noise is that we tend to forget that they aren't just inferior prototypes of ourselves with inefficient energy conversion systems dedicated to reproduction."

"So let's talk price," Jeeves transmitted, sensing that his desirability as a customer was peaking. "It's a start-up operation with limited capital, but they're planning on expanding into a full line of cross-species fashions."

"It's been done before," Ug replied. "My records show a surge in cross-species fashions every time new biologicals claw their way up off their planet of origin."

"But they don't know that," Jeeves pointed out. "They don't remember."

"You give us this job at our standard setup rate and guaranty me first refusal on new products for the next thousand cycles, I'll do the first run of hats for the cost of materials," Ug offered.

"How much for setting up the production line?"

"Thirty thousand Stryx creds, but any engineering change orders from these plans will be billable hours," the artificial person said.

"You aren't giving your services away," Jeeves grumbled, but he made the transfer from his internal currency holder and the amount immediately popped up in an ornate frame on the artificial person's ceiling. "You hacked your register to make a display?"

"I do it with mirrors," Ug admitted. "Sometimes while I'm in the box recharging it's nice to look at the latest deposit. Reminds me why I'm exercising the electrons. Hey, I recognize the company name on the transfer—SBJ Auctioneers. One of the Chintoo groups that got burned by a fashion cycle while trying to manufacture on their own account got stuck with a bunch of stretchy products for Drazens and disposed of the unsold inventory through your firm."

"We barely broke even on those," Jeeves said. "It did give me a chance to see how adaptable my human partners can be. By the end of the auction, they were cutting up Drazen tentacle warmers and selling them to human retailers as various sizes of knee and elbow sleeves for athletes. Well, I better head back and give the girls the good news. You wouldn't believe how impatient biologicals can be."

"How'd you choose me?" Ug transmitted out of curiosity as Jeeves turned to exit. "There are bigger cooperatives than mine on Chintoo and I know you were concerned about timing."

"A human-derived artificial person who spent time as a graphics designer here suggested you. He did some work on a collection of monogrammed bath towels you produce for the cruise lines."

"The one who left to become a spy? How's that going for him?"

"He's having a ball," Jeeves replied. "They currently have him working undercover as a newspaper reporter to keep an eye on Grenouthian agents working undercover for the bunny news networks. Humans are a hoot once you get to know them, especially when they're trying to be serious."

The relatively primitive Sharf AI and the young Stryx exchanged an electronic handshake, and Jeeves exited the orbital for open space. After a quick look around to fix his position in the galaxy, he began calculating his route back to Union Station. The unaccustomed exercise in multiverse math gave him an idea for a new business, but he doubted his elders would be amused.

EarthCent Ambassador Series:


Date Night on Union Station

Alien Night on Union Station

High Priest on Union Station

Spy Night on Union Station

Carnival on Union Station

Wanderers on Union Station

Vacation on Union Station

Guest Night on Union Station

Word Night on Union Station

Party Night on Union Station

Review Night on Union Station

Family Night on Union Station

Book Night on Union Station

LARP Night on Union Station

## About the Author

E. M. Foner lives in Northampton, MA with an imaginary German Shepherd who's been trained to bite bankers. The author welcomes reader comments at e_foner@yahoo.com.

You can sign up for new book announcements on the author's website - IfItBreaks.com

CPSIA information can be obtained
at www.ICGtesting.com
Printed in the USA
BVHW041344110522
636711BV00002B/235